ANN M. MARTIN

THE BABY-SITTERS CLUB

MARY ANNE SAVES THE DAY

A GRAPHIC NOVEL BY

RAINA TELGEMEIER

WITH COLOR BY BRADEN LAMB

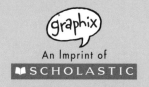

graphix

An Imprint of

SCHOLASTIC

Library of Congress Control Number: 2015935841

ISBN 978-0-545-88617-8 (hardcover)
ISBN 978-0-545-88621-5 (paperback)

10 9 8 7 6 5 4 3 2 1   15 16 17 18 19

Printed in Singapore 46
First color edition printing, November 2015

Lettering by John Green
Edited by David Levithan, Sheila Keenan, and Cassandra Pelham
Book design by Phil Falco
Creative Director: David Saylor

This book is for Beth McKeever Perkins, my old baby-sitting buddy.
With Love (and years of memories)
A. M. M.

Thanks to David Saylor, Cassandra Pelham, Ellie Berger,
Marion Vitus, Alisa Harris, Alison Wilgus, Zack Giallongo, Steve Flack,
Phil Falco, Braden Lamb, and John Green. And of course, thanks to my
husband, Dave Roman, for always encouraging me to do my best.
R. T.

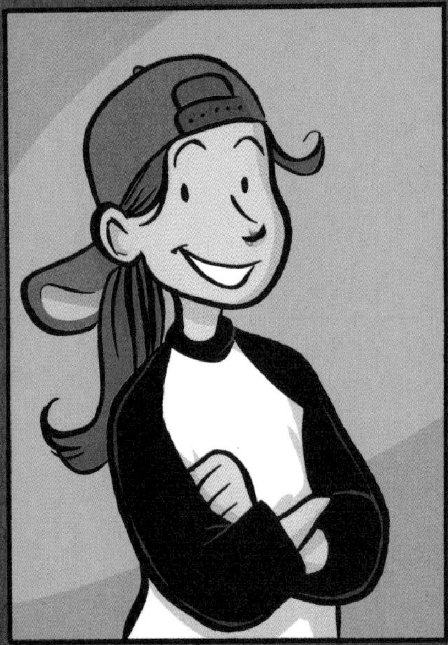

KRISTY THOMAS
PRESIDENT

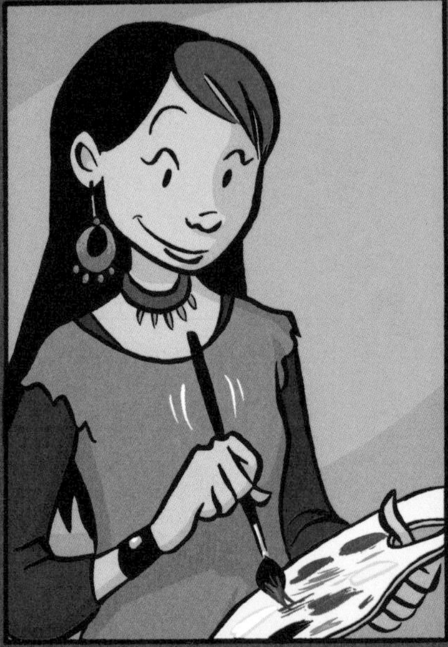

CLAUDIA KISHI
VICE PRESIDENT

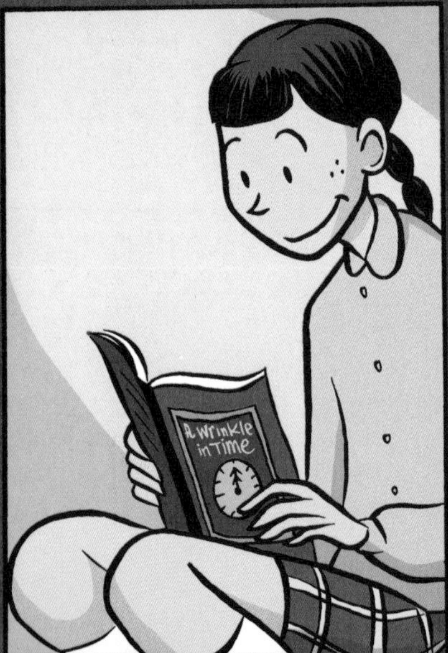
A Wrinkle in Time

MARY ANNE SPIER
SECRETARY

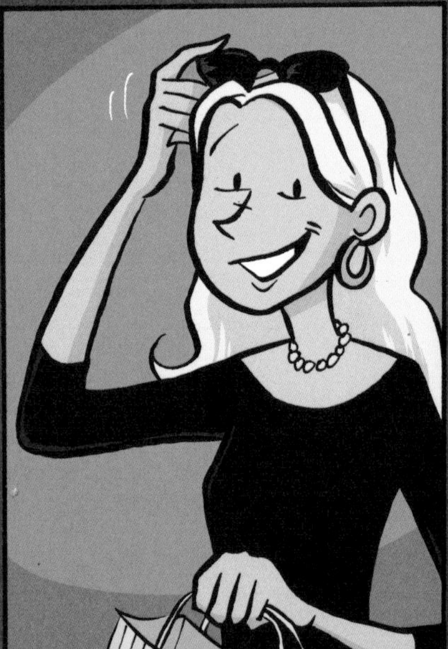

STACEY MCGILL
TREASURER

CHAPTER 1

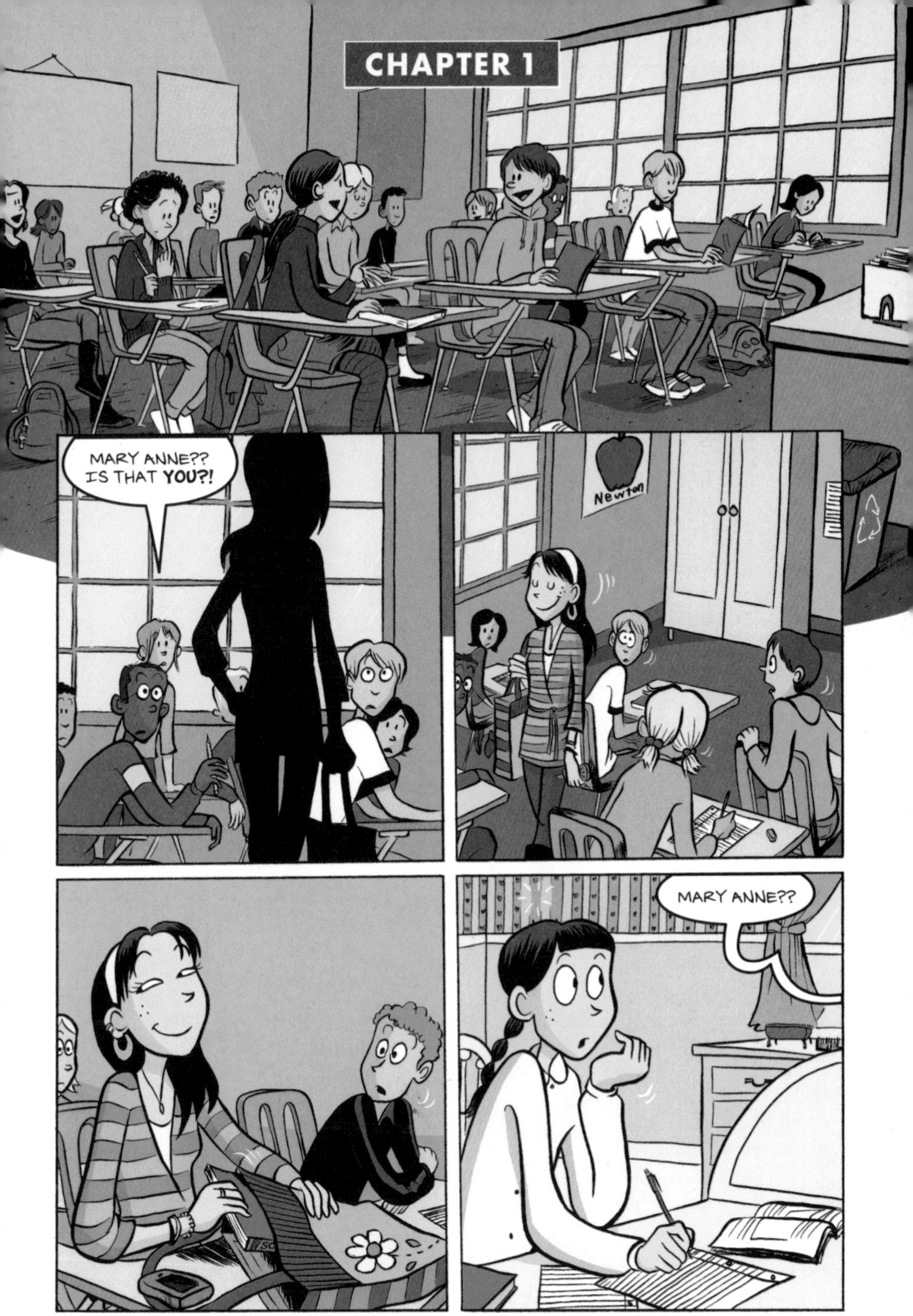
MARY ANNE?? IS THAT YOU?!
Newton
MARY ANNE??

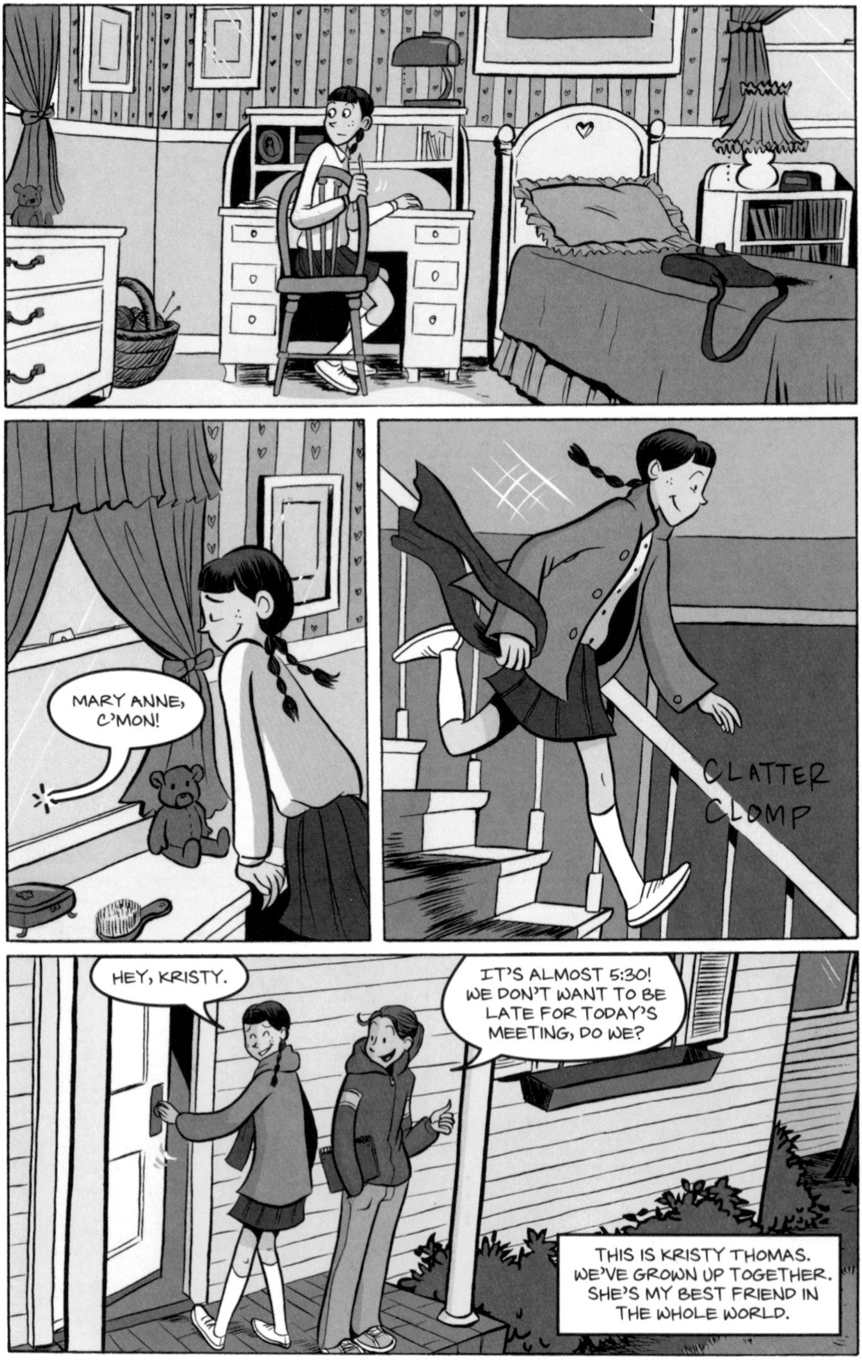
MARY ANNE, C'MON!
CLATTER
CLOMP
HEY, KRISTY.
IT'S ALMOST 5:30! WE DON'T WANT TO BE LATE FOR TODAY'S MEETING, DO WE?
THIS IS KRISTY THOMAS. WE'VE GROWN UP TOGETHER. SHE'S MY BEST FRIEND IN THE WHOLE WORLD.

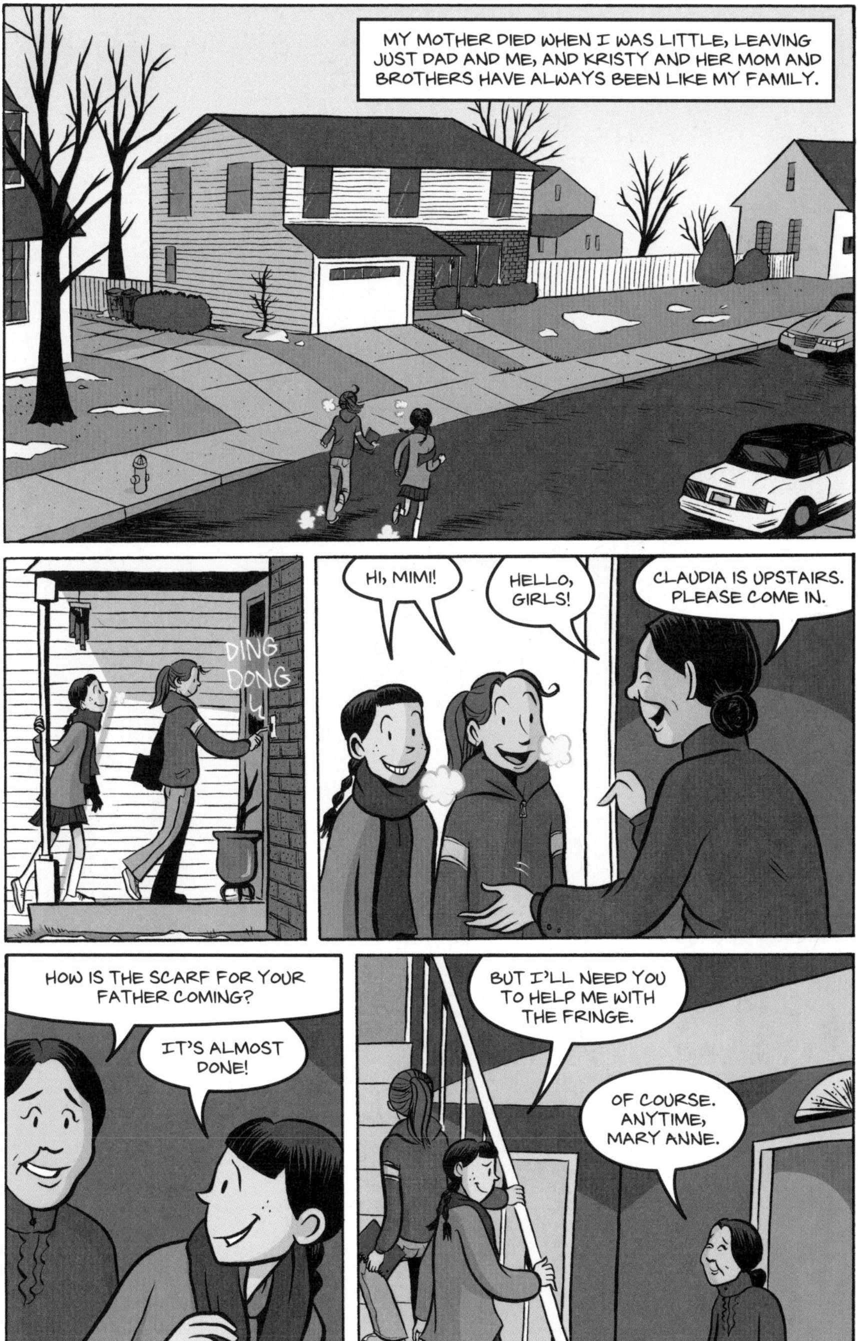
MY MOTHER DIED WHEN I WAS LITTLE, LEAVING JUST DAD AND ME, AND KRISTY AND HER MOM AND BROTHERS HAVE ALWAYS BEEN LIKE MY FAMILY.
DING DONG
HI, MIMI!
HELLO, GIRLS!
CLAUDIA IS UPSTAIRS. PLEASE COME IN.
HOW IS THE SCARF FOR YOUR FATHER COMING?
IT'S ALMOST DONE!
BUT I'LL NEED YOU TO HELP ME WITH THE FRINGE.
OF COURSE. ANYTIME, MARY ANNE.

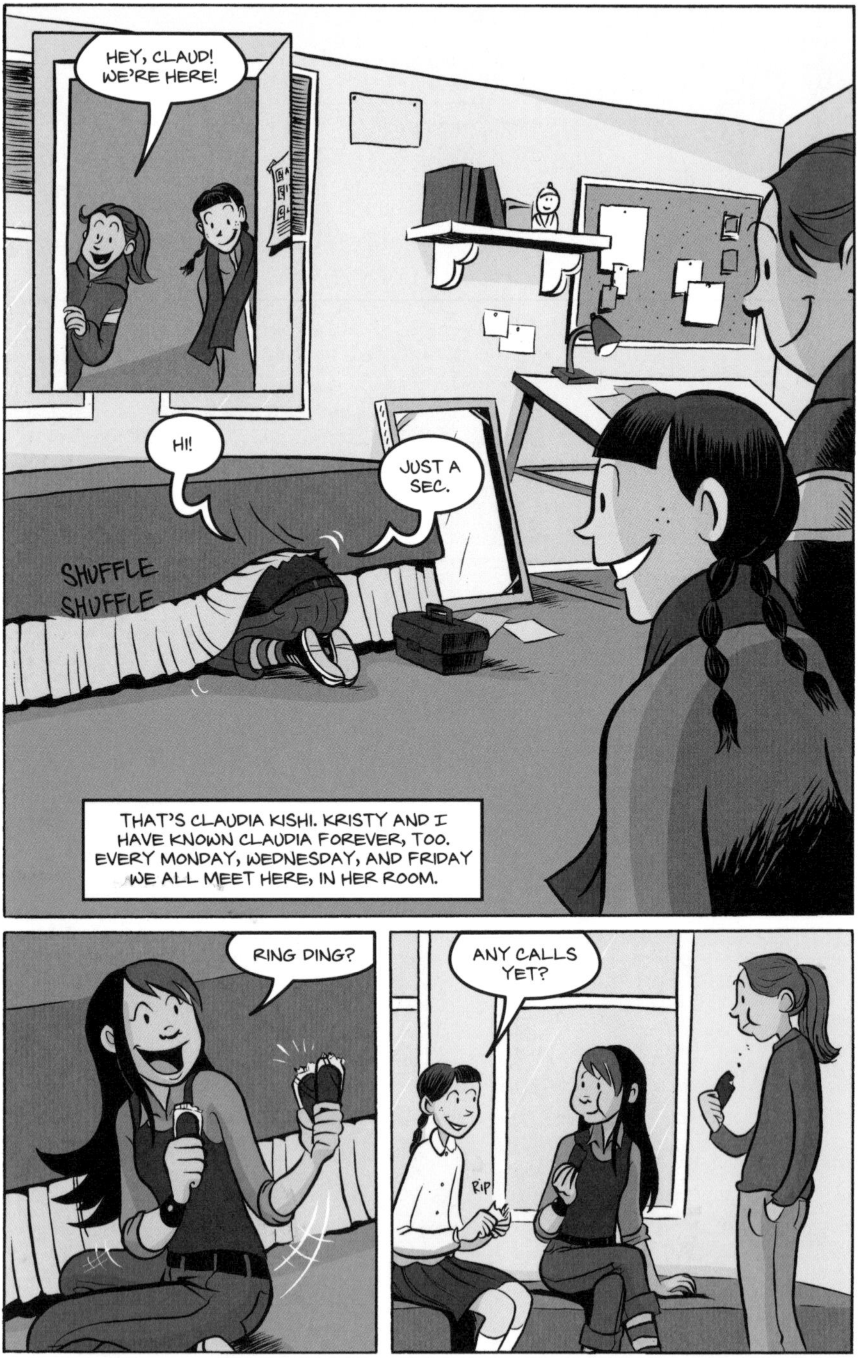
HEY, CLAUD! WE'RE HERE!
HI!
JUST A SEC.
SHUFFLE SHUFFLE
THAT'S CLAUDIA KISHI. KRISTY AND I HAVE KNOWN CLAUDIA FOREVER, TOO. EVERY MONDAY, WEDNESDAY, AND FRIDAY WE ALL MEET HERE, IN HER ROOM.
RING DING?
ANY CALLS YET?
RIP

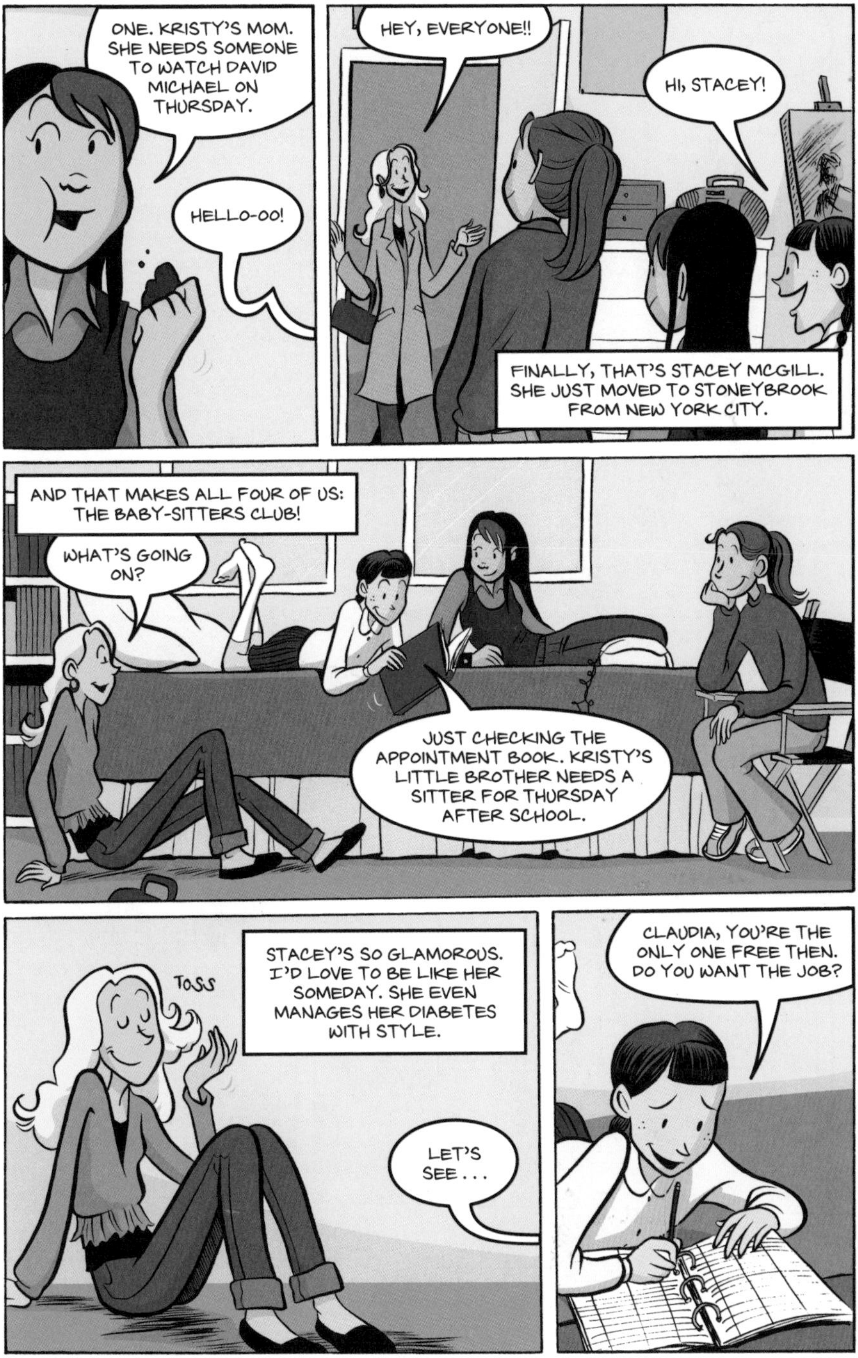
ONE. KRISTY'S MOM. SHE NEEDS SOMEONE TO WATCH DAVID MICHAEL ON THURSDAY.
HELLO-OO!
HEY, EVERYONE!!
HI, STACEY!
FINALLY, THAT'S STACEY MCGILL. SHE JUST MOVED TO STONEYBROOK FROM NEW YORK CITY.
AND THAT MAKES ALL FOUR OF US: THE BABY-SITTERS CLUB!
WHAT'S GOING ON?
JUST CHECKING THE APPOINTMENT BOOK. KRISTY'S LITTLE BROTHER NEEDS A SITTER FOR THURSDAY AFTER SCHOOL.
STACEY'S SO GLAMOROUS. I'D LOVE TO BE LIKE HER SOMEDAY. SHE EVEN MANAGES HER DIABETES WITH STYLE.
TOSS
LET'S SEE . . .
CLAUDIA, YOU'RE THE ONLY ONE FREE THEN. DO YOU WANT THE JOB?

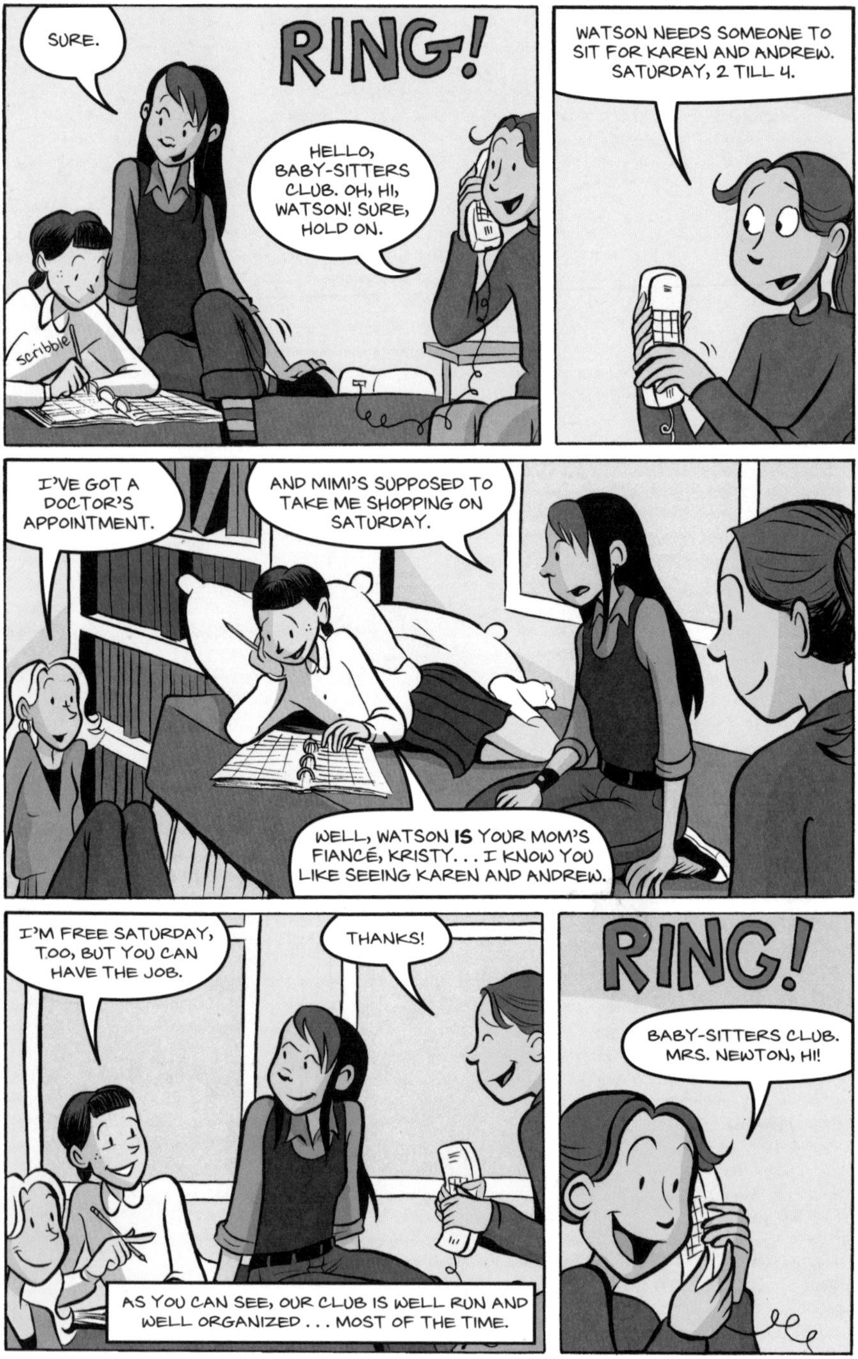
SURE.
RING!
HELLO, BABY-SITTERS CLUB. OH, HI, WATSON! SURE, HOLD ON.
scribble
WATSON NEEDS SOMEONE TO SIT FOR KAREN AND ANDREW. SATURDAY, 2 TILL 4.
I'VE GOT A DOCTOR'S APPOINTMENT.
AND MIMI'S SUPPOSED TO TAKE ME SHOPPING ON SATURDAY.
WELL, WATSON **IS** YOUR MOM'S FIANCÉ, KRISTY. . . I KNOW YOU LIKE SEEING KAREN AND ANDREW.
I'M FREE SATURDAY, T.OO, BUT YOU CAN HAVE THE JOB.
THANKS!
AS YOU CAN SEE, OUR CLUB IS WELL RUN AND WELL ORGANIZED . . . MOST OF THE TIME.
RING!
BABY-SITTERS CLUB. MRS. NEWTON, HI!

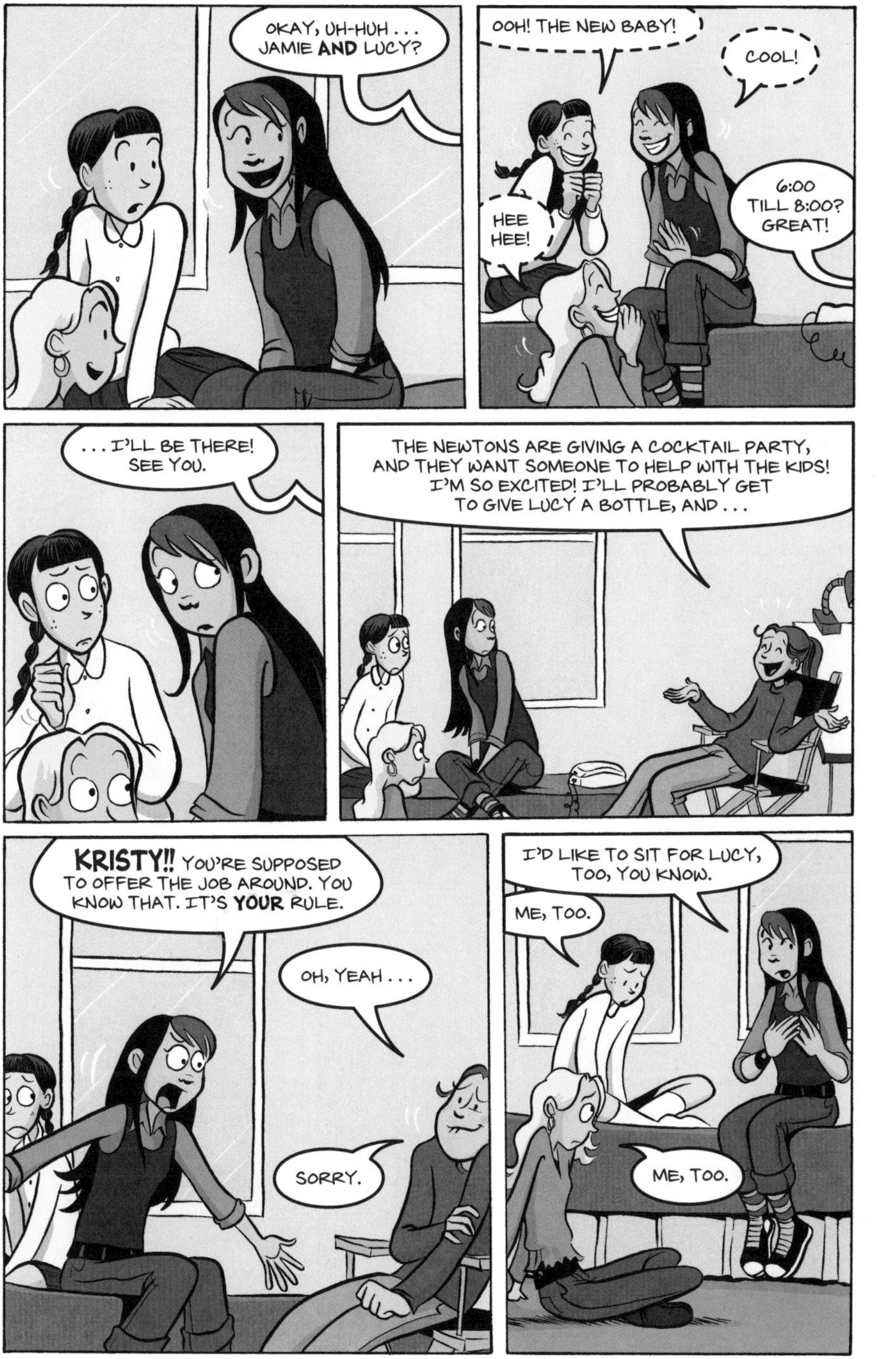
OKAY, UH-HUH . . . JAMIE AND LUCY?
OOH! THE NEW BABY!
COOL!
HEE HEE!
6:00 TILL 8:00? GREAT!
. . . I'LL BE THERE! SEE YOU.
THE NEWTONS ARE GIVING A COCKTAIL PARTY, AND THEY WANT SOMEONE TO HELP WITH THE KIDS! I'M SO EXCITED! I'LL PROBABLY GET TO GIVE LUCY A BOTTLE, AND . . .
KRISTY!! YOU'RE SUPPOSED TO OFFER THE JOB AROUND. YOU KNOW THAT. IT'S YOUR RULE.
OH, YEAH . . .
SORRY.
I'D LIKE TO SIT FOR LUCY, TOO, YOU KNOW.
ME, TOO.
ME, TOO.

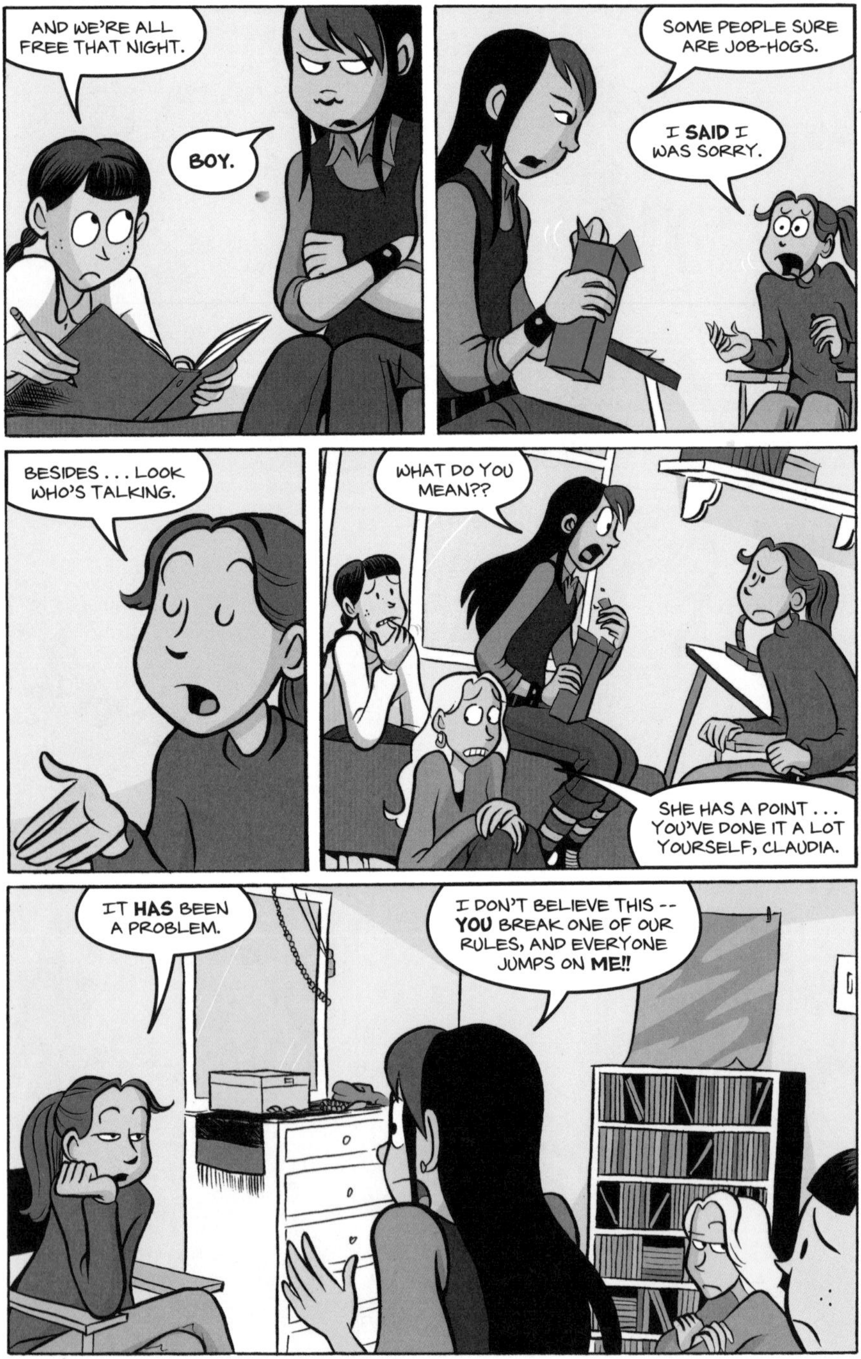
AND WE'RE ALL FREE THAT NIGHT.
BOY.
SOME PEOPLE SURE ARE JOB-HOGS.
I **SAID** I WAS SORRY.
BESIDES . . . LOOK WHO'S TALKING.
WHAT DO YOU MEAN??
SHE HAS A POINT . . . YOU'VE DONE IT A LOT YOURSELF, CLAUDIA.
IT **HAS** BEEN A PROBLEM.
I DON'T BELIEVE THIS -- **YOU** BREAK ONE OF OUR RULES, AND EVERYONE JUMPS ON **ME!!**

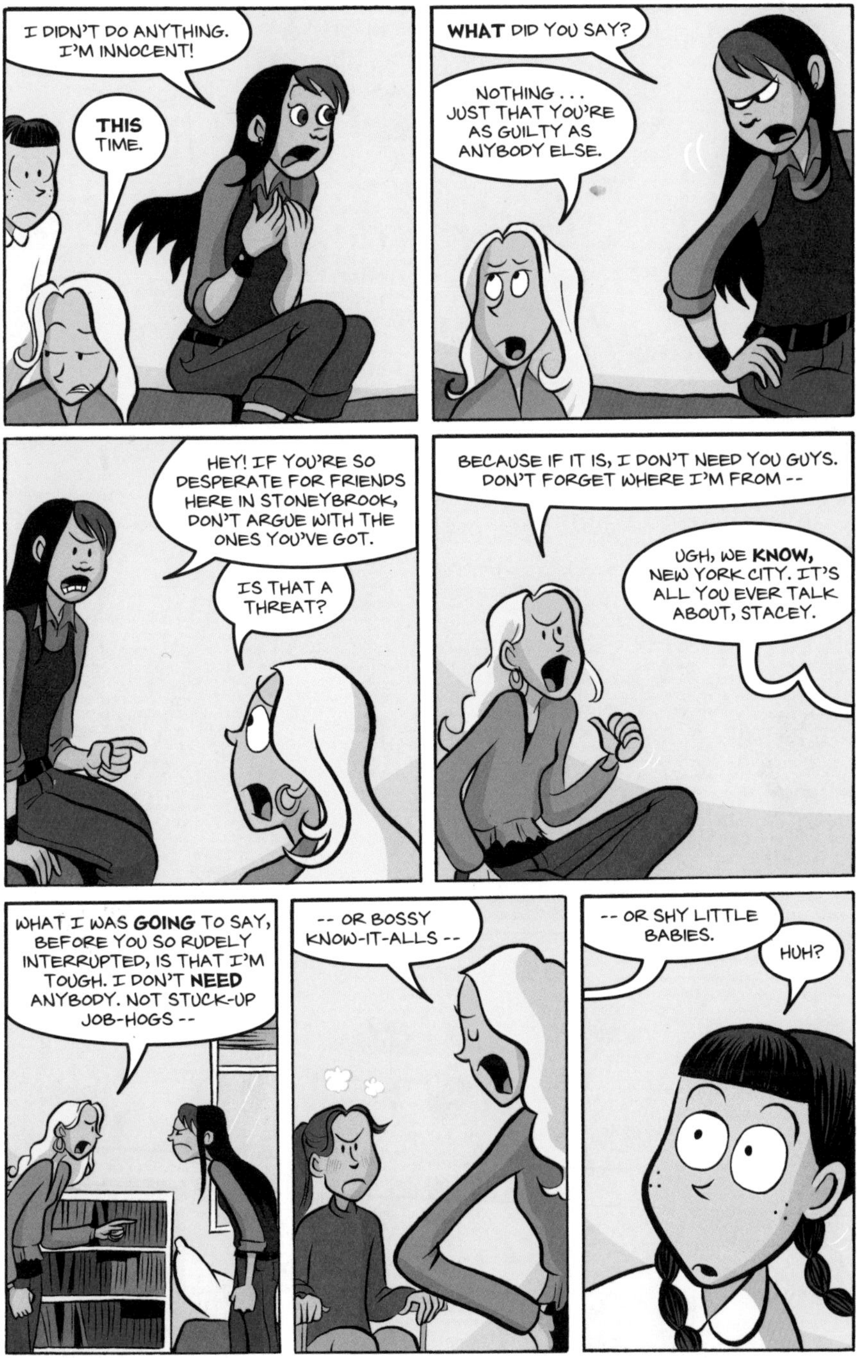
I DIDN'T DO ANYTHING. I'M INNOCENT!
THIS TIME.
WHAT DID YOU SAY?
NOTHING . . . JUST THAT YOU'RE AS GUILTY AS ANYBODY ELSE.
HEY! IF YOU'RE SO DESPERATE FOR FRIENDS HERE IN STONEYBROOK, DON'T ARGUE WITH THE ONES YOU'VE GOT.
IS THAT A THREAT?
BECAUSE IF IT IS, I DON'T NEED YOU GUYS. DON'T FORGET WHERE I'M FROM --
UGH, WE KNOW, NEW YORK CITY. IT'S ALL YOU EVER TALK ABOUT, STACEY.
WHAT I WAS GOING TO SAY, BEFORE YOU SO RUDELY INTERRUPTED, IS THAT I'M TOUGH. I DON'T NEED ANYBODY. NOT STUCK-UP JOB-HOGS --
-- OR BOSSY KNOW-IT-ALLS --
-- OR SHY LITTLE BABIES.
HUH?

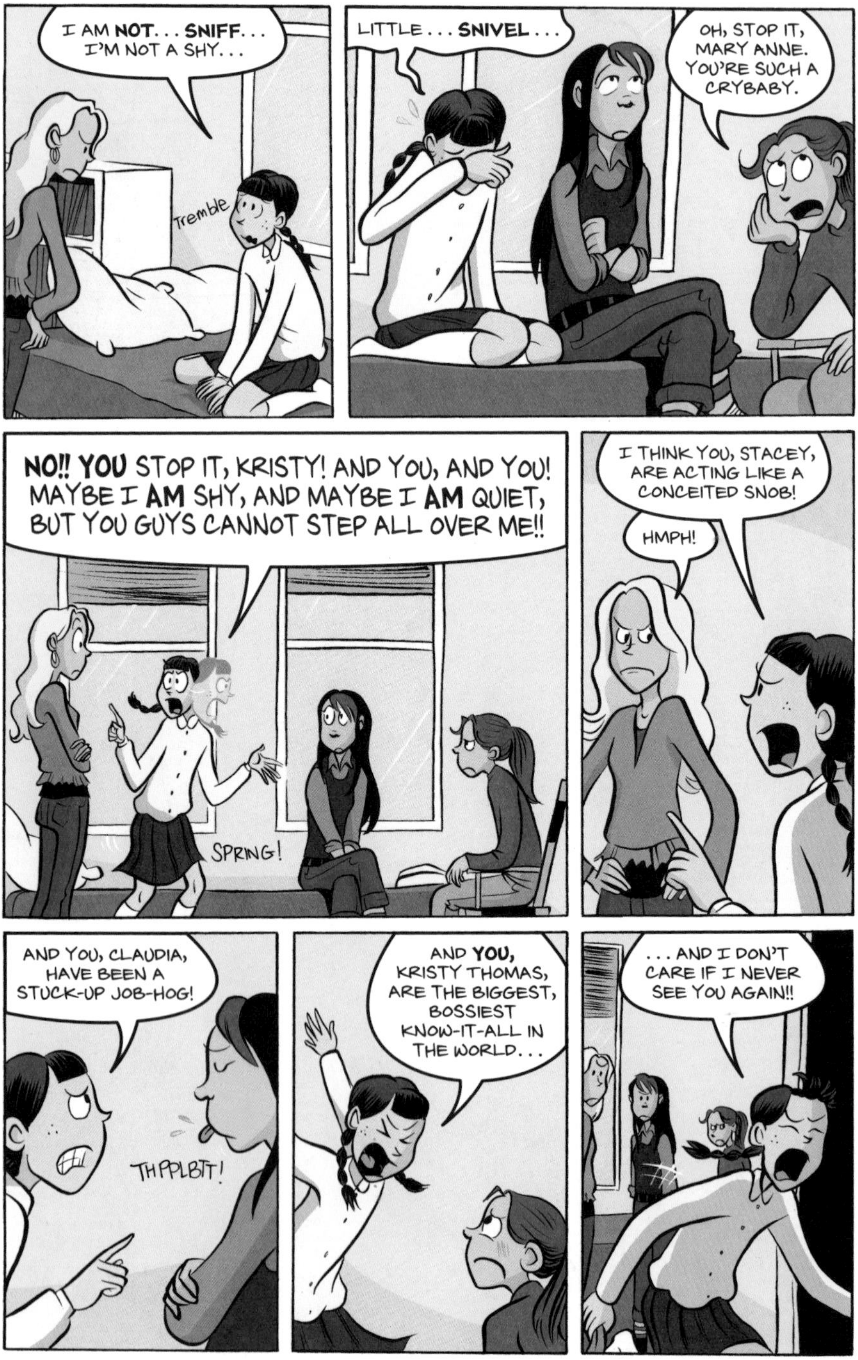

I AM **NOT**. . . **SNIFF**. . . I'M NOT A SHY. . .
Tremble
LITTLE. . . **SNIVEL**. . .
OH, STOP IT, MARY ANNE. YOU'RE SUCH A CRYBABY.
NO!! YOU STOP IT, KRISTY! AND YOU, AND YOU! MAYBE I **AM** SHY, AND MAYBE I **AM** QUIET, BUT YOU GUYS CANNOT STEP ALL OVER ME!!
SPRING!
I THINK YOU, STACEY, ARE ACTING LIKE A CONCEITED SNOB!
HMPH!
AND YOU, CLAUDIA, HAVE BEEN A STUCK-UP JOB-HOG!
THPPLBTT!
AND **YOU,** KRISTY THOMAS, ARE THE BIGGEST, BOSSIEST KNOW-IT-ALL IN THE WORLD. . .
. . . AND I DON'T CARE IF I NEVER SEE YOU AGAIN!!

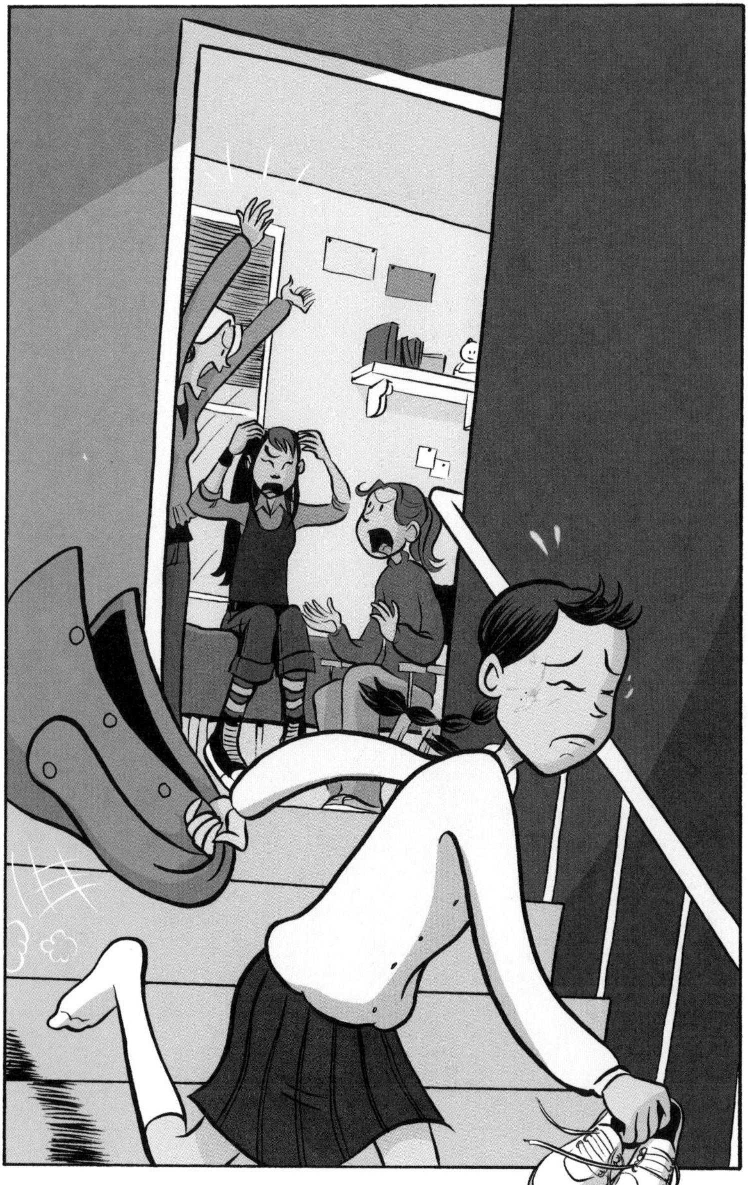

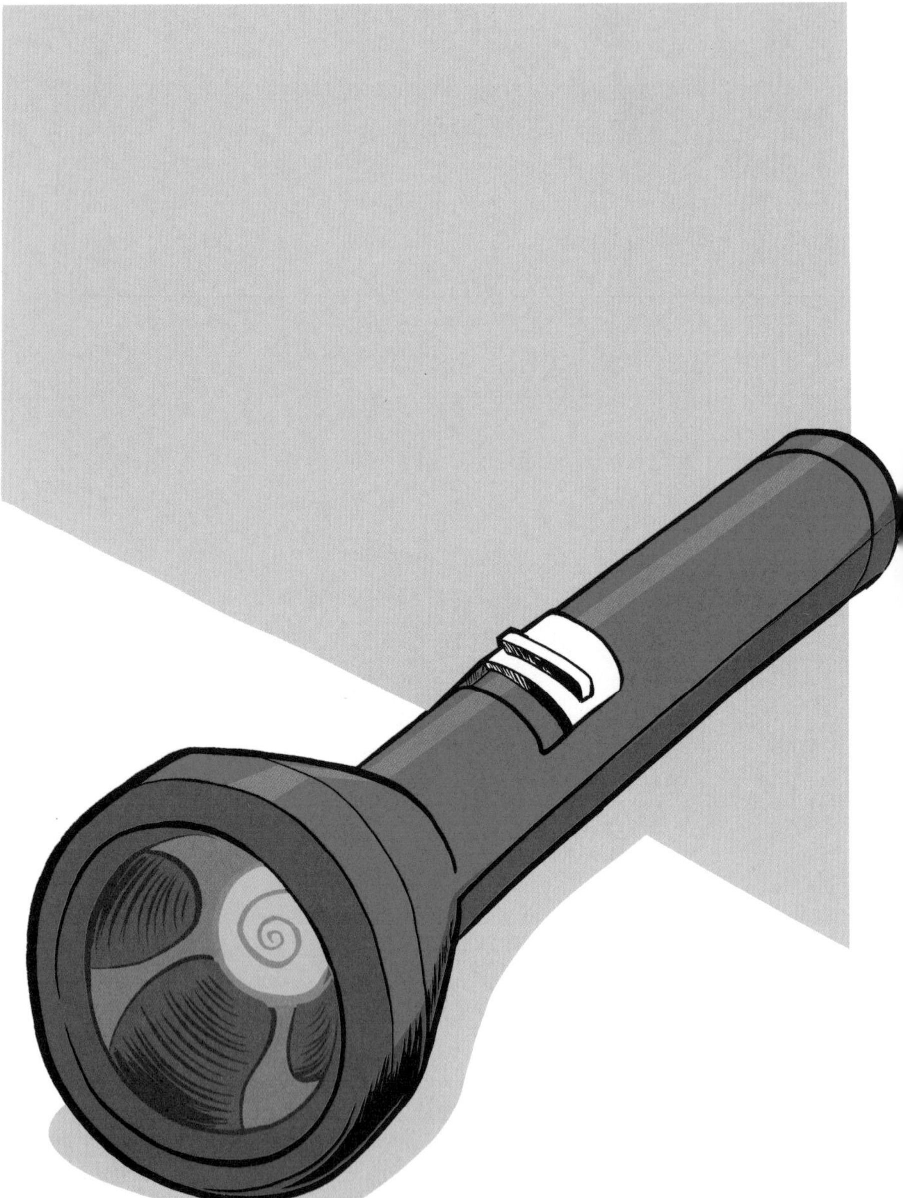

CHAPTER 2

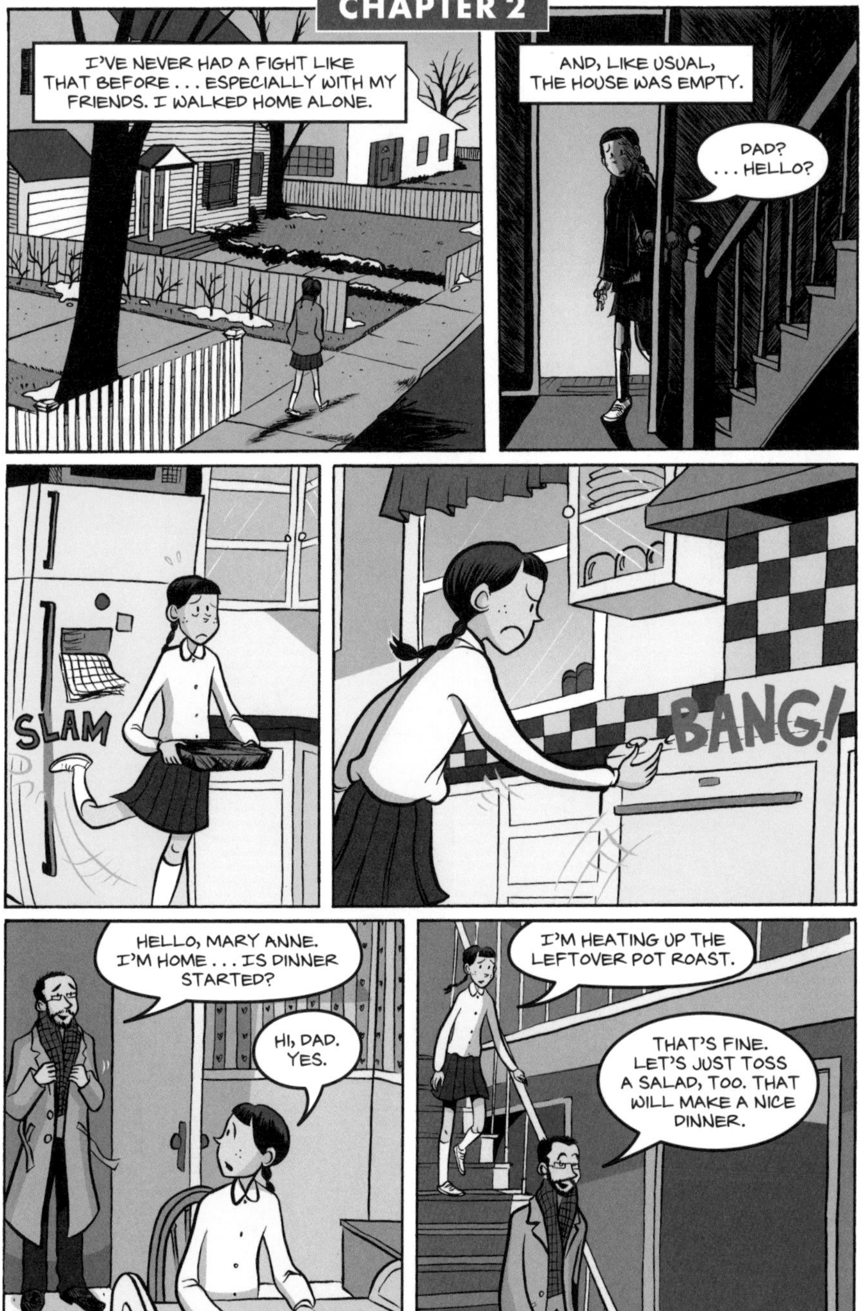
I'VE NEVER HAD A FIGHT LIKE THAT BEFORE . . . ESPECIALLY WITH MY FRIENDS. I WALKED HOME ALONE.
AND, LIKE USUAL, THE HOUSE WAS EMPTY.
DAD? . . . HELLO?
SLAM
BANG!
HELLO, MARY ANNE. I'M HOME . . . IS DINNER STARTED?
HI, DAD. YES.
I'M HEATING UP THE LEFTOVER POT ROAST.
THAT'S FINE. LET'S JUST TOSS A SALAD, TOO. THAT WILL MAKE A NICE DINNER.

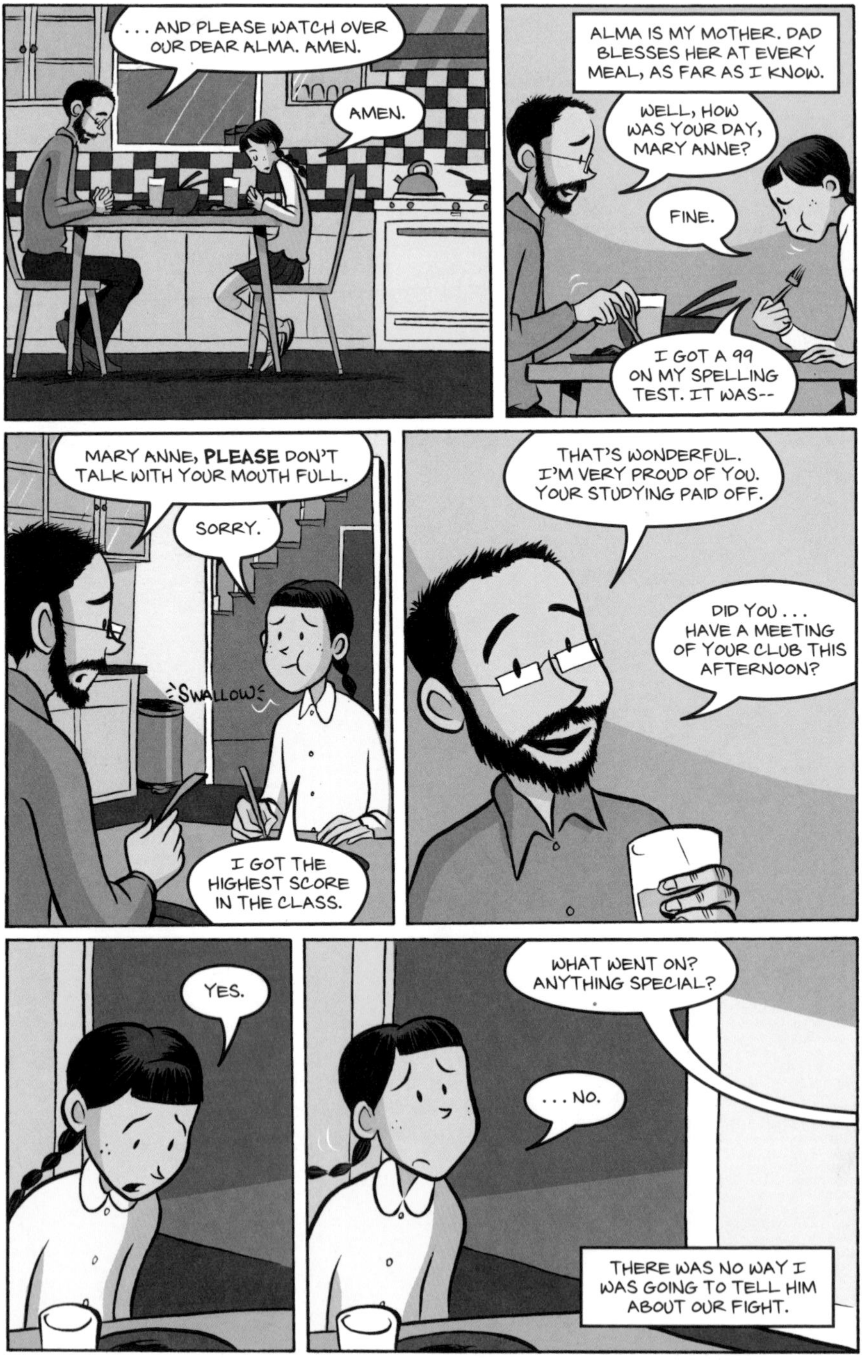
. . . AND PLEASE WATCH OVER OUR DEAR ALMA. AMEN.
AMEN.
ALMA IS MY MOTHER. DAD BLESSES HER AT EVERY MEAL, AS FAR AS I KNOW.
WELL, HOW WAS YOUR DAY, MARY ANNE?
FINE.
I GOT A 99 ON MY SPELLING TEST. IT WAS--
MARY ANNE, **PLEASE** DON'T TALK WITH YOUR MOUTH FULL.
SORRY.
SWALLOW
I GOT THE HIGHEST SCORE IN THE CLASS.
THAT'S WONDERFUL. I'M VERY PROUD OF YOU. YOUR STUDYING PAID OFF.
DID YOU . . . HAVE A MEETING OF YOUR CLUB THIS AFTERNOON?
YES.
WHAT WENT ON? ANYTHING SPECIAL?
. . . NO.
THERE WAS NO WAY I WAS GOING TO TELL HIM ABOUT OUR FIGHT.

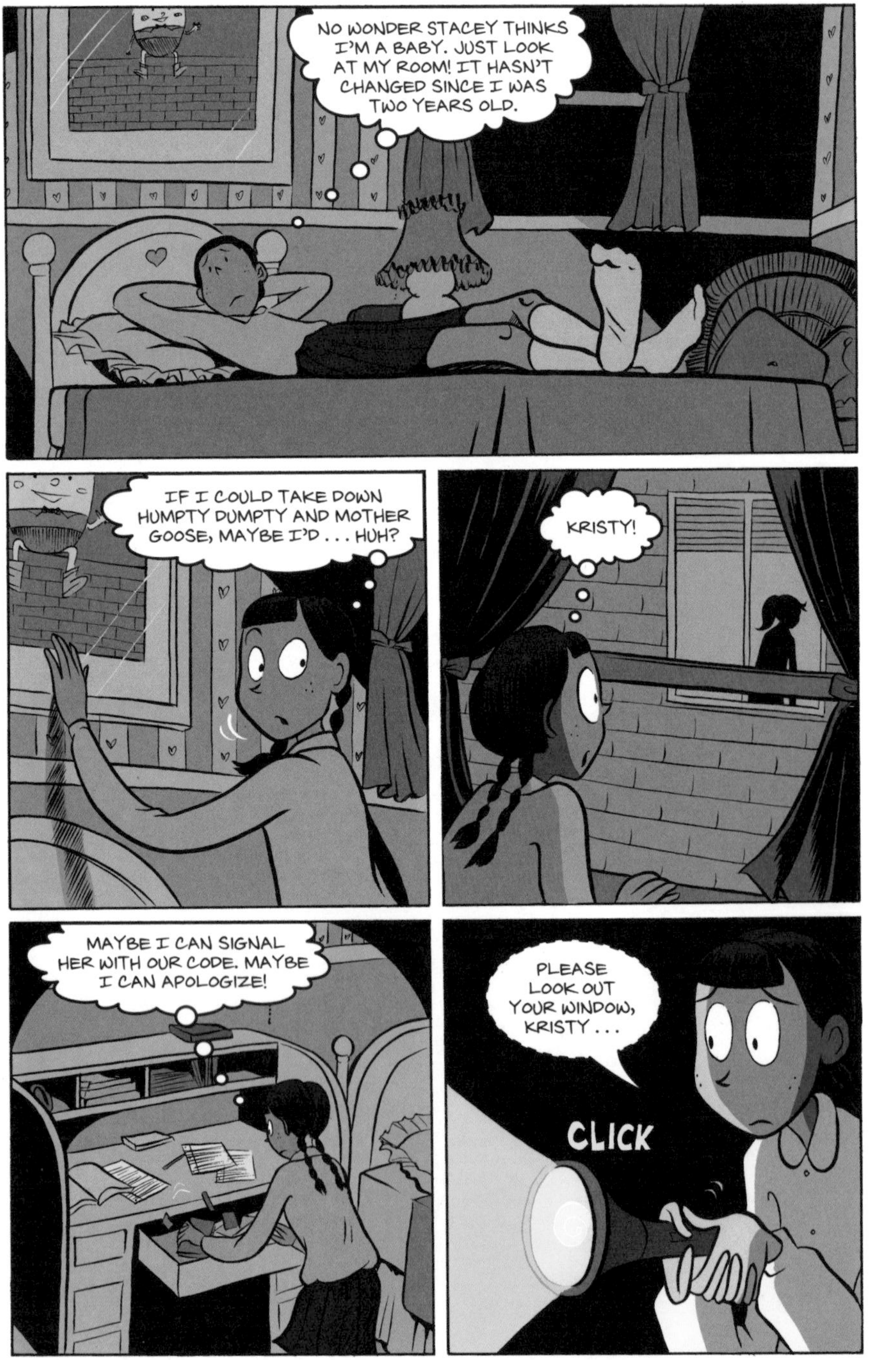
NO WONDER STACEY THINKS I'M A BABY. JUST LOOK AT MY ROOM! IT HASN'T CHANGED SINCE I WAS TWO YEARS OLD.
IF I COULD TAKE DOWN HUMPTY DUMPTY AND MOTHER GOOSE, MAYBE I'D . . . HUH?
KRISTY!
MAYBE I CAN SIGNAL HER WITH OUR CODE. MAYBE I CAN APOLOGIZE!
PLEASE LOOK OUT YOUR WINDOW, KRISTY . . .
CLICK

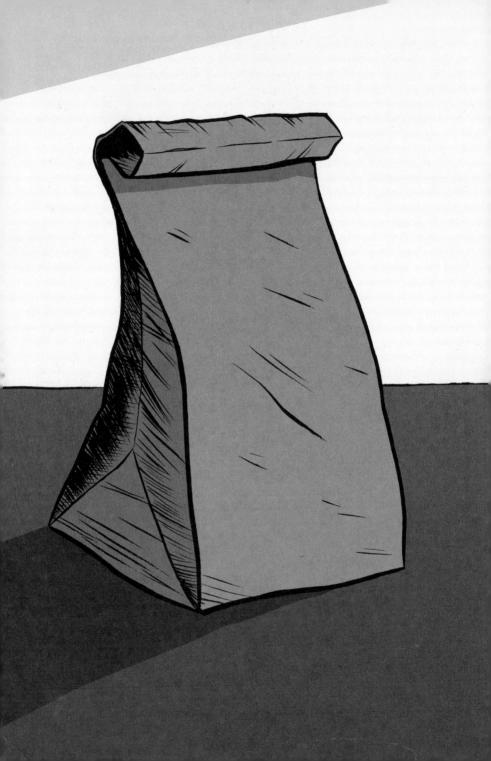

CHAPTER 3

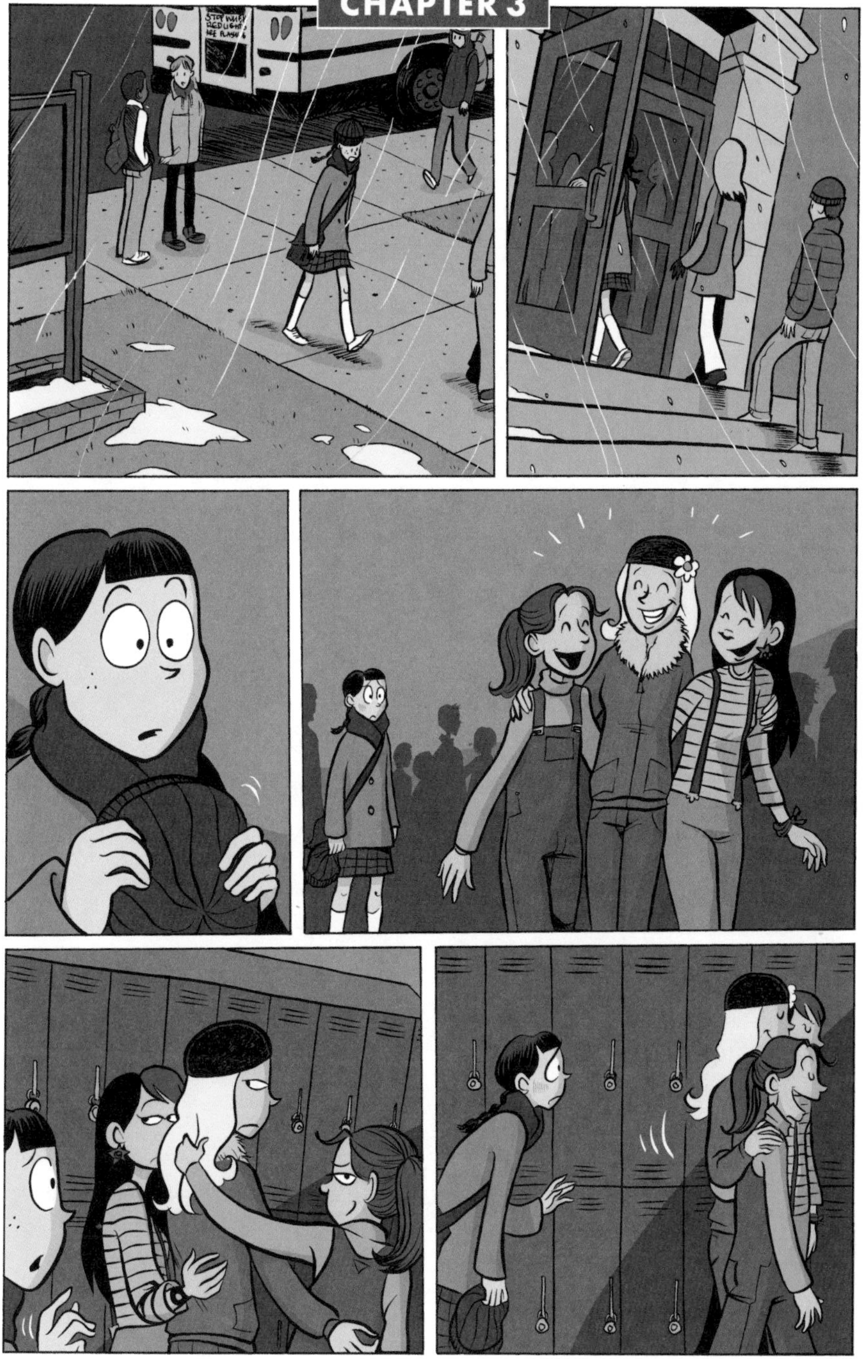

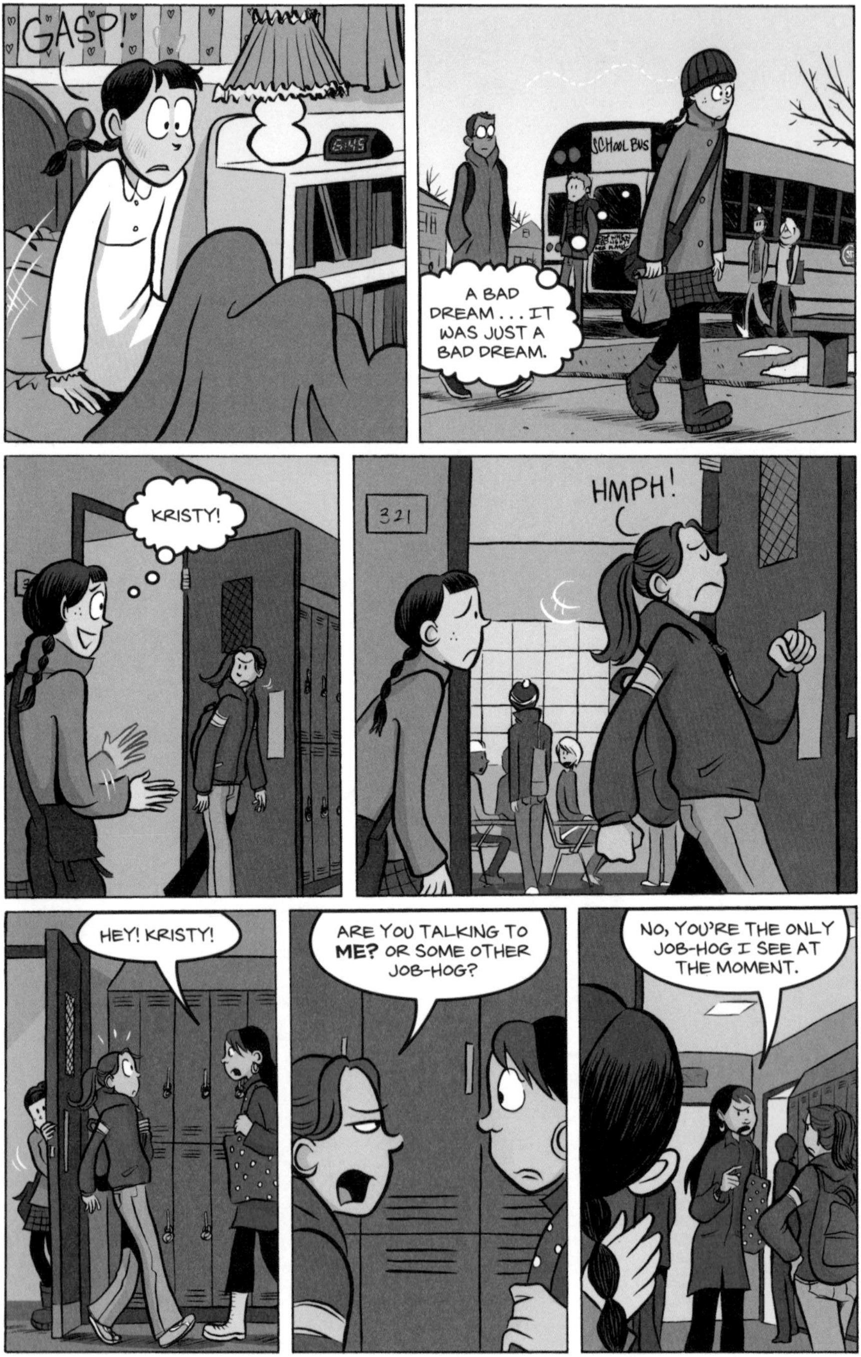
GASP!
A BAD DREAM . . . IT WAS JUST A BAD DREAM.
KRISTY!
HMPH!
HEY! KRISTY!
ARE YOU TALKING TO **ME?** OR SOME OTHER JOB-HOG?
NO, YOU'RE THE ONLY JOB-HOG I SEE AT THE MOMENT.

22

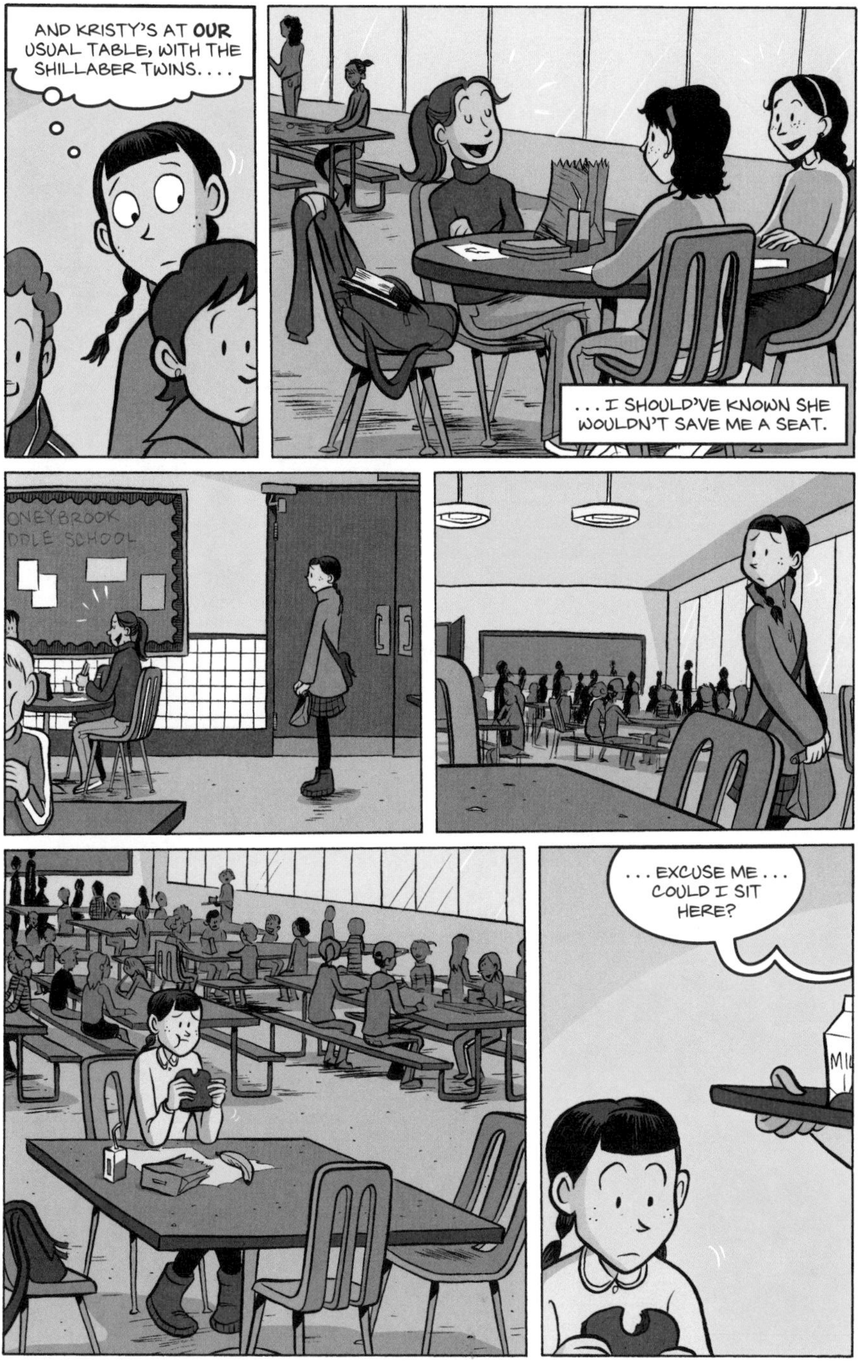
AND KRISTY'S AT **OUR** USUAL TABLE, WITH THE SHILLABER TWINS....
...I SHOULD'VE KNOWN SHE WOULDN'T SAVE ME A SEAT.
...EXCUSE ME... COULD I SIT HERE?

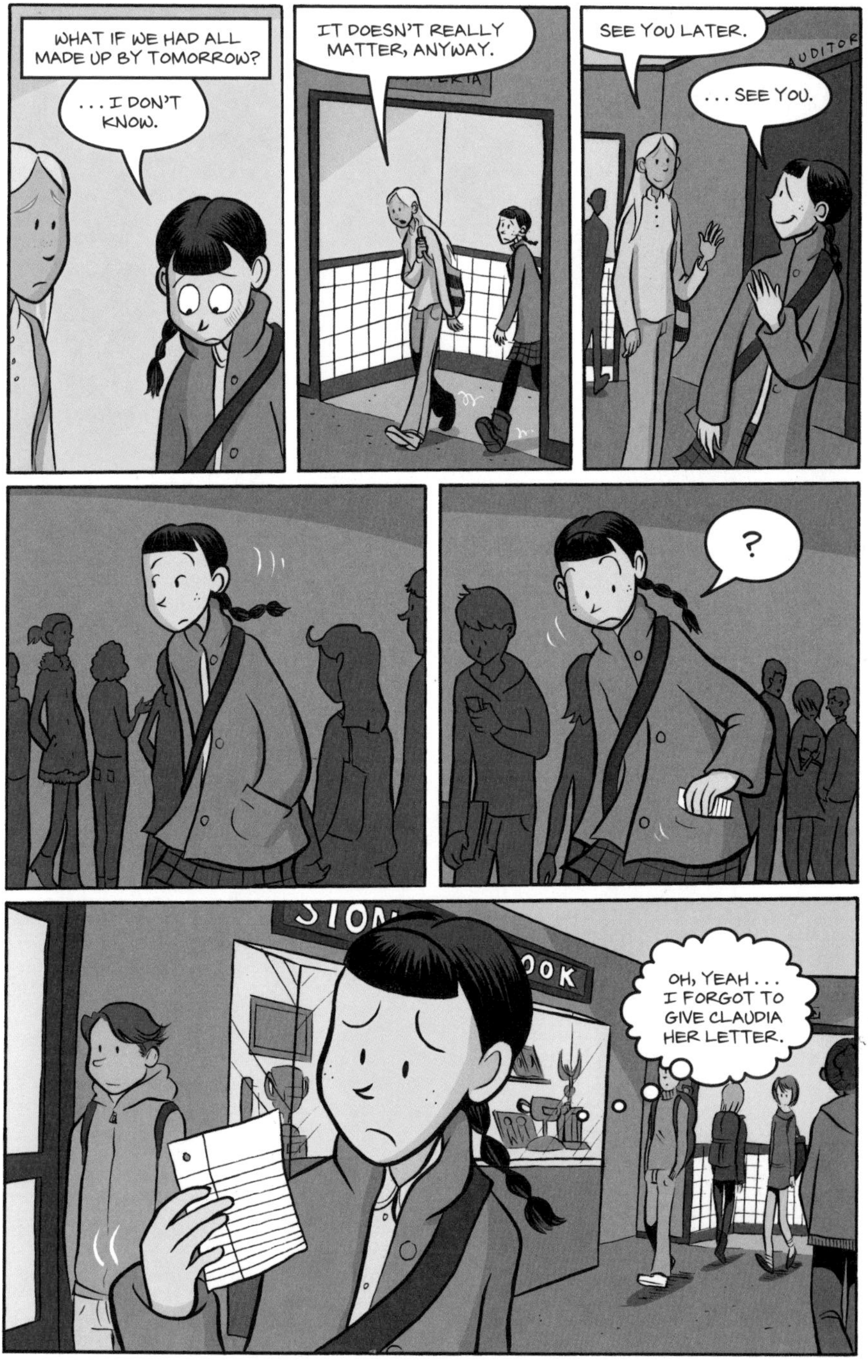
WHAT IF WE HAD ALL MADE UP BY TOMORROW?
. . . I DON'T KNOW.
IT DOESN'T REALLY MATTER, ANYWAY.
SEE YOU LATER.
AUDITOR
. . . SEE YOU.
?
OH, YEAH . . . I FORGOT TO GIVE CLAUDIA HER LETTER.

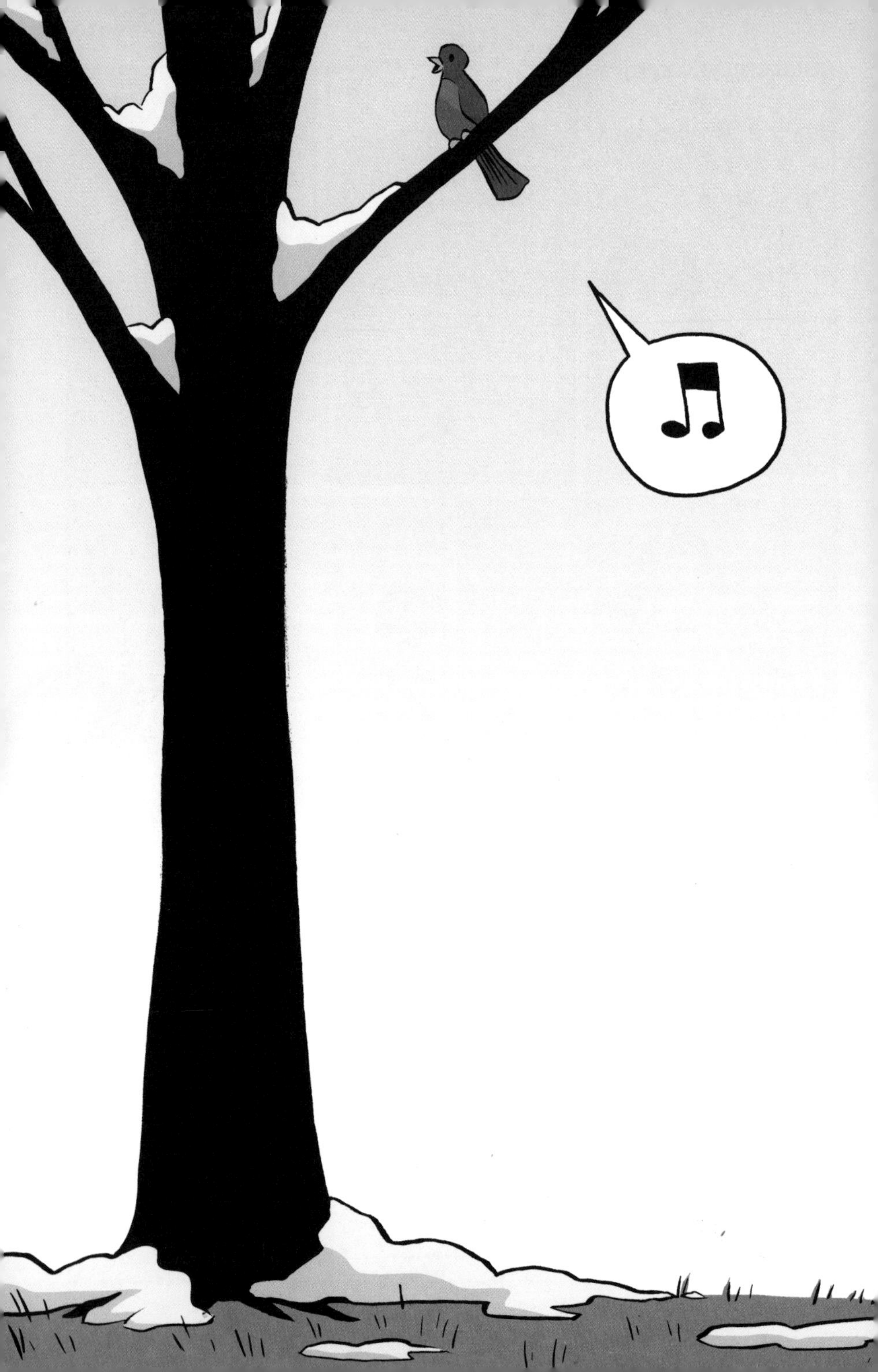

30

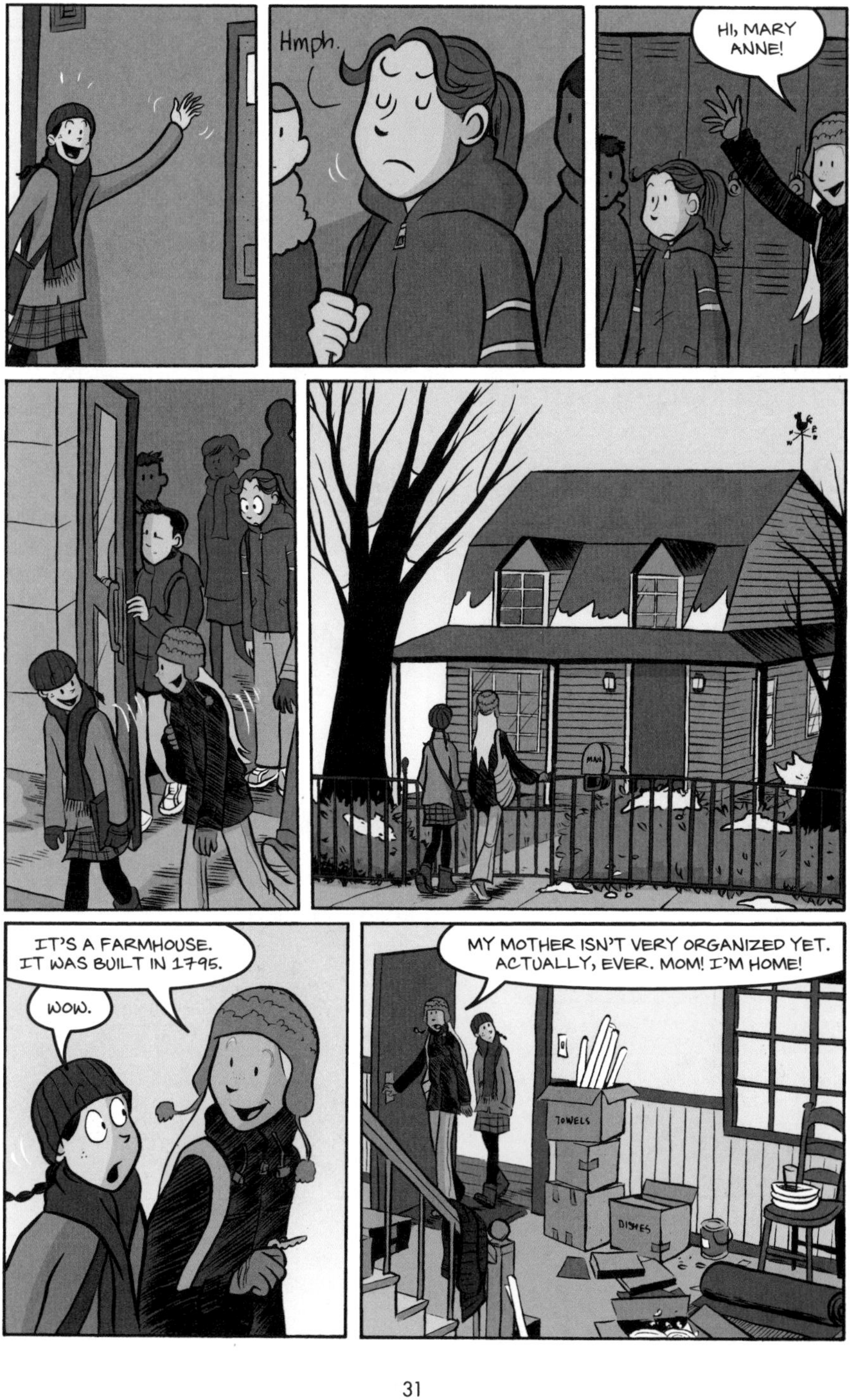
Hmph.
HI, MARY ANNE!
IT'S A FARMHOUSE. IT WAS BUILT IN 1795.
WOW.
MY MOTHER ISN'T VERY ORGANIZED YET. ACTUALLY, EVER. MOM! I'M HOME!
TOWELS
DISHES

32

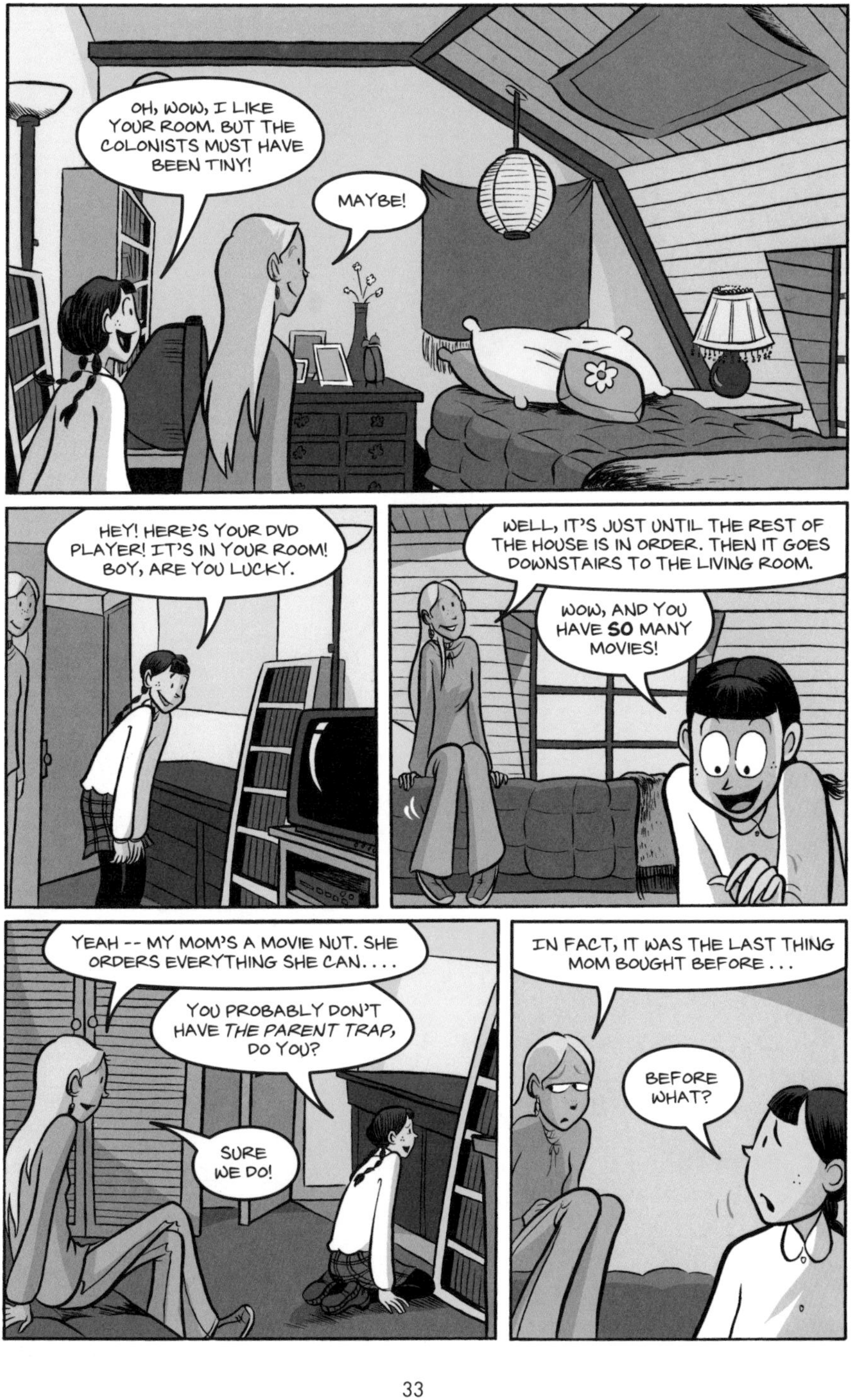
OH, WOW, I LIKE YOUR ROOM. BUT THE COLONISTS MUST HAVE BEEN TINY!
MAYBE!
HEY! HERE'S YOUR DVD PLAYER! IT'S IN YOUR ROOM! BOY, ARE YOU LUCKY.
WELL, IT'S JUST UNTIL THE REST OF THE HOUSE IS IN ORDER. THEN IT GOES DOWNSTAIRS TO THE LIVING ROOM.
WOW, AND YOU HAVE **SO** MANY MOVIES!
YEAH -- MY MOM'S A MOVIE NUT. SHE ORDERS EVERYTHING SHE CAN. . . .
YOU PROBABLY DON'T HAVE *THE PARENT TRAP*, DO YOU?
SURE WE DO!
IN FACT, IT WAS THE LAST THING MOM BOUGHT BEFORE . . .
BEFORE WHAT?

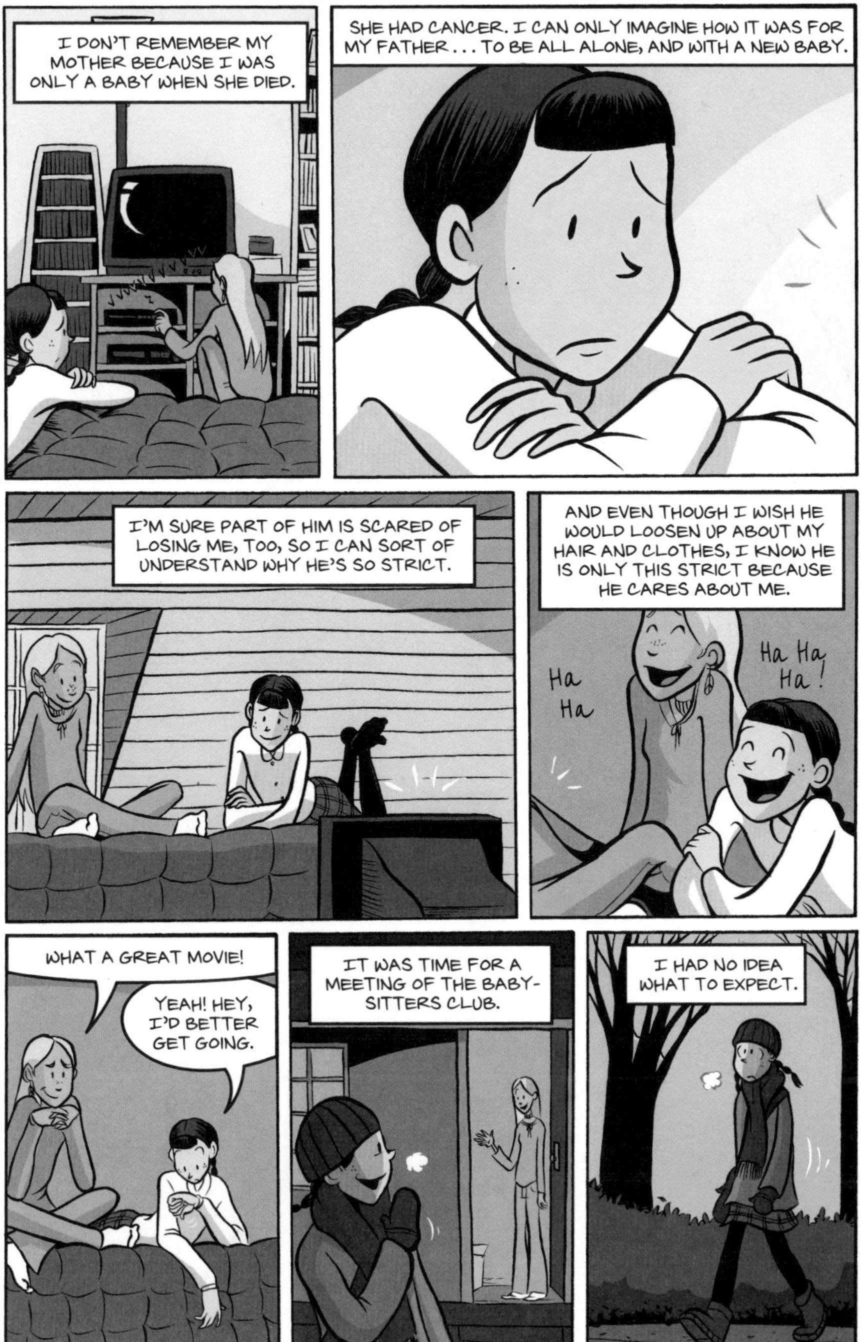

I DON'T REMEMBER MY MOTHER BECAUSE I WAS ONLY A BABY WHEN SHE DIED.
SHE HAD CANCER. I CAN ONLY IMAGINE HOW IT WAS FOR MY FATHER . . . TO BE ALL ALONE, AND WITH A NEW BABY.
I'M SURE PART OF HIM IS SCARED OF LOSING ME, TOO, SO I CAN SORT OF UNDERSTAND WHY HE'S SO STRICT.
AND EVEN THOUGH I WISH HE WOULD LOOSEN UP ABOUT MY HAIR AND CLOTHES, I KNOW HE IS ONLY THIS STRICT BECAUSE HE CARES ABOUT ME.
Ha Ha
Ha Ha Ha!
WHAT A GREAT MOVIE!
YEAH! HEY, I'D BETTER GET GOING.
IT WAS TIME FOR A MEETING OF THE BABY-SITTERS CLUB.
I HAD NO IDEA WHAT TO EXPECT.

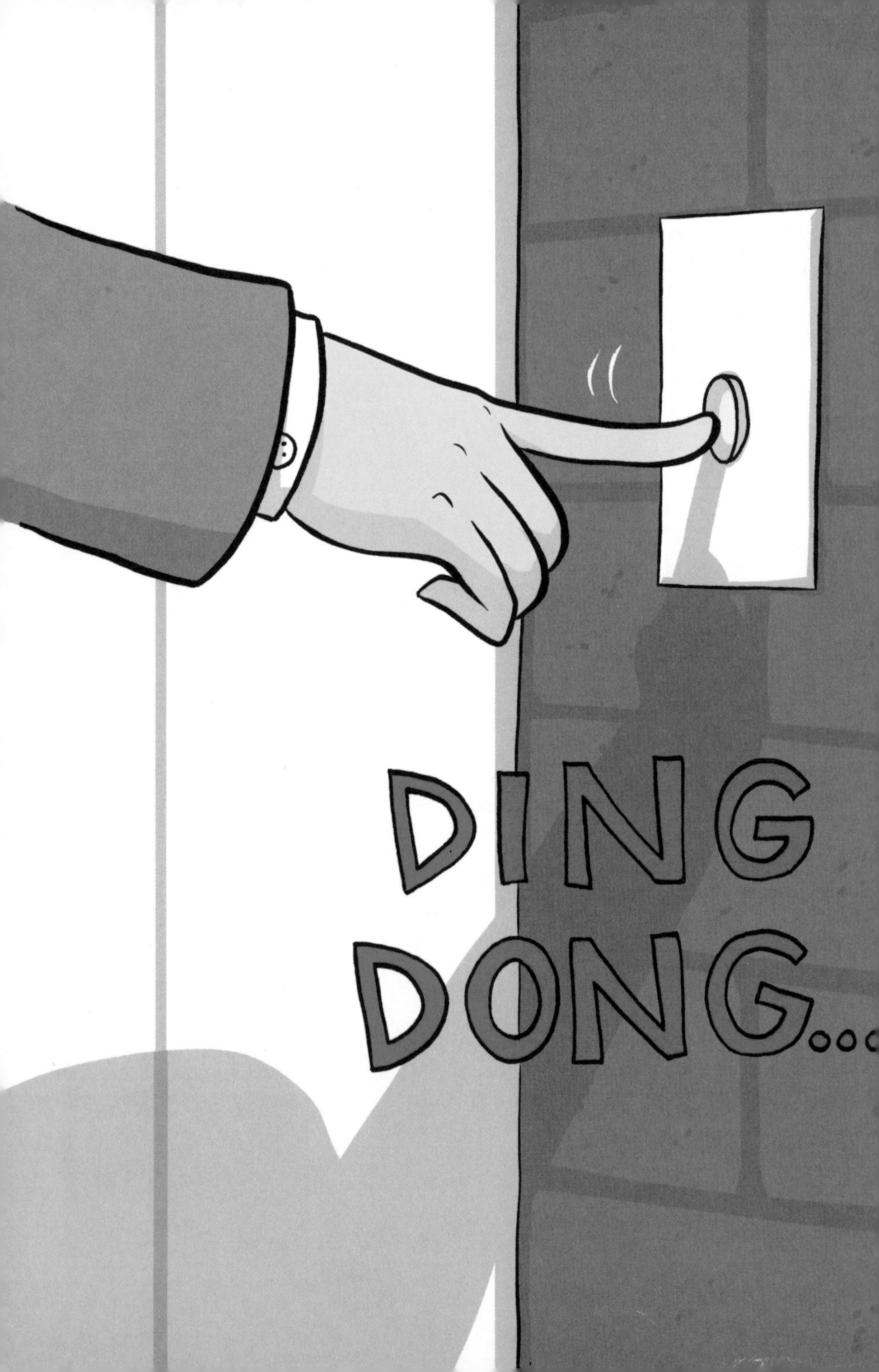
DING
DONG...

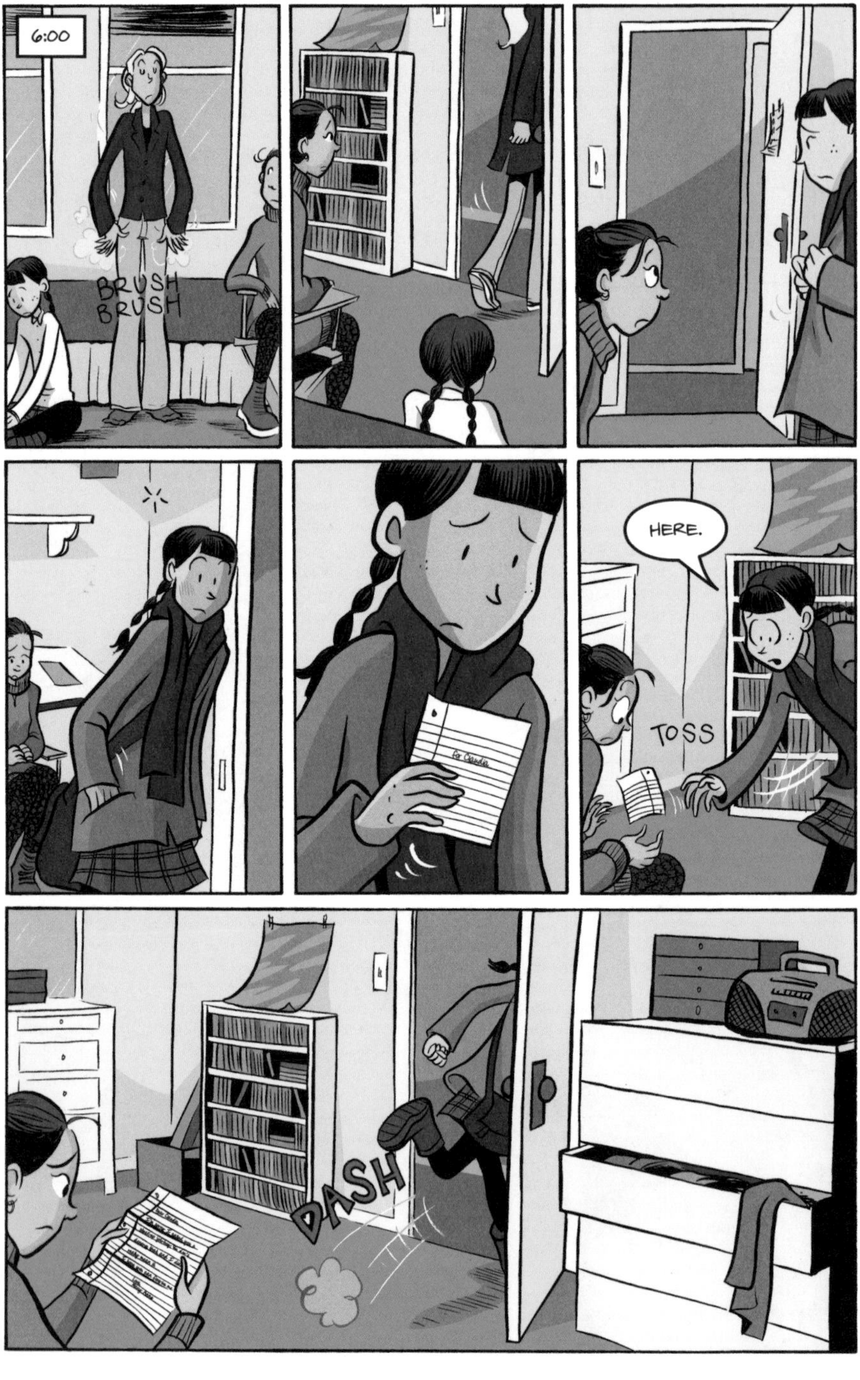
6:00
BRUSH
BRUSH
HERE.
TOSS
DASH

CHAPTER 5

41

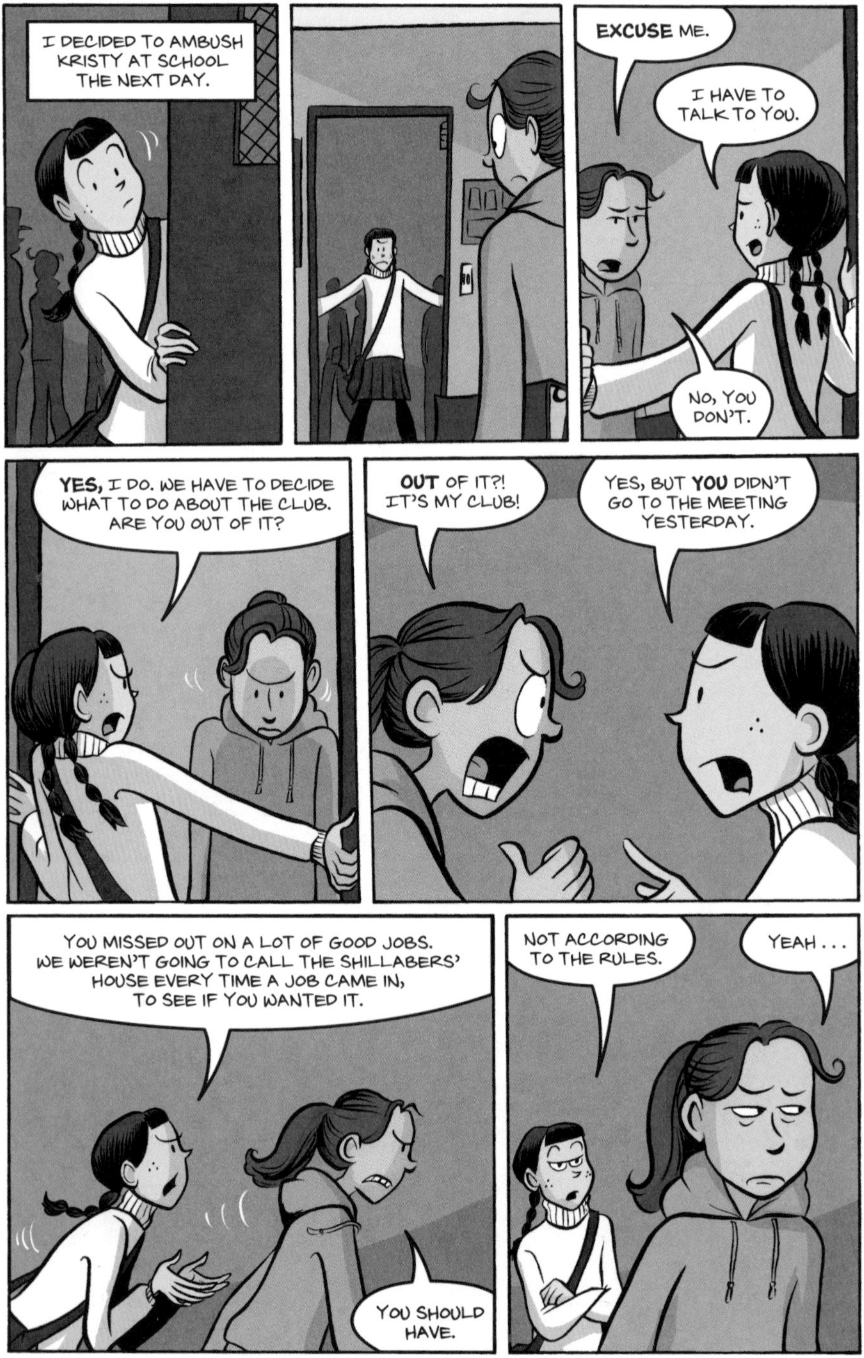
I DECIDED TO AMBUSH KRISTY AT SCHOOL THE NEXT DAY.
EXCUSE ME.
I HAVE TO TALK TO YOU.
NO, YOU DON'T.
YES, I DO. WE HAVE TO DECIDE WHAT TO DO ABOUT THE CLUB. ARE YOU OUT OF IT?
OUT OF IT?! IT'S MY CLUB!
YES, BUT YOU DIDN'T GO TO THE MEETING YESTERDAY.
YOU MISSED OUT ON A LOT OF GOOD JOBS. WE WEREN'T GOING TO CALL THE SHILLABERS' HOUSE EVERY TIME A JOB CAME IN, TO SEE IF YOU WANTED IT.
YOU SHOULD HAVE.
NOT ACCORDING TO THE RULES.
YEAH . . .

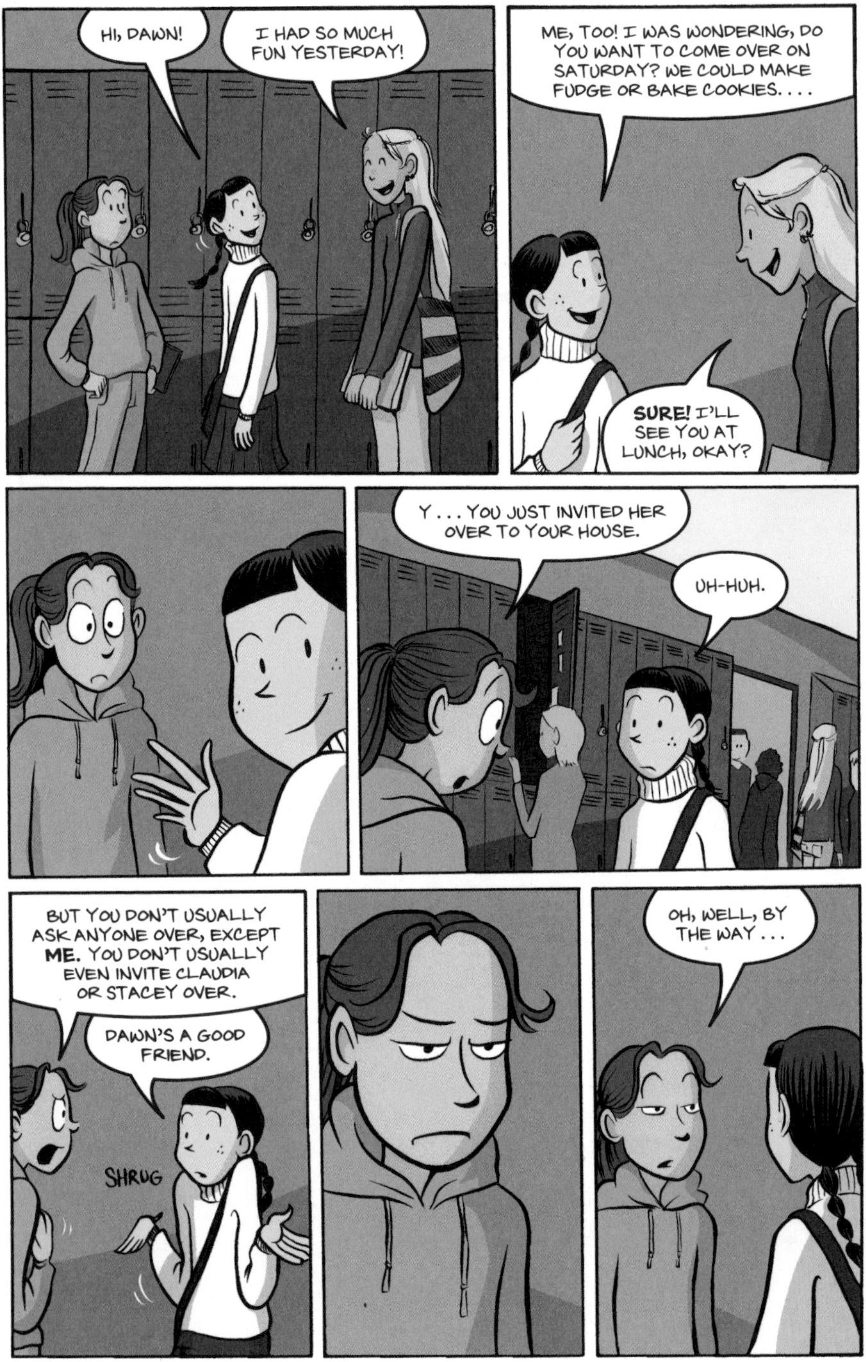
HI, DAWN!
I HAD SO MUCH FUN YESTERDAY!
ME, TOO! I WAS WONDERING, DO YOU WANT TO COME OVER ON SATURDAY? WE COULD MAKE FUDGE OR BAKE COOKIES. . . .
SURE! I'LL SEE YOU AT LUNCH, OKAY?
Y . . . YOU JUST INVITED HER OVER TO YOUR HOUSE.
UH-HUH.
BUT YOU DON'T USUALLY ASK ANYONE OVER, EXCEPT **ME.** YOU DON'T USUALLY EVEN INVITE CLAUDIA OR STACEY OVER.
DAWN'S A GOOD FRIEND.
SHRUG
OH, WELL, BY THE WAY . . .

Sunday, January 11

This afternoon, I sat for Jenny Prezzioso. Jenny
is three. She's the Pikes' neighbor, so I had met
her a few times before today. She and her parents
both look very prim and proper but Mrs. Prezzioso
is the only one who acts that way. She looks like
she just stepped out of the pages of a magazine.
And she dresses Jenny as if every day were Easter
Sunday: frilly dresses, lacy socks, and ribbons
in her hair. Mrs. P probably thinks "jeans" is
a dirty word.

Mr. P, on the other hand, looks like he'd rather be
dozing in front of the TV in sweats, a T-shirt, and
mismatched socks. And Jenny tries hard, but she just
isn't what her mother wants her to be. . . .

Stacey

49

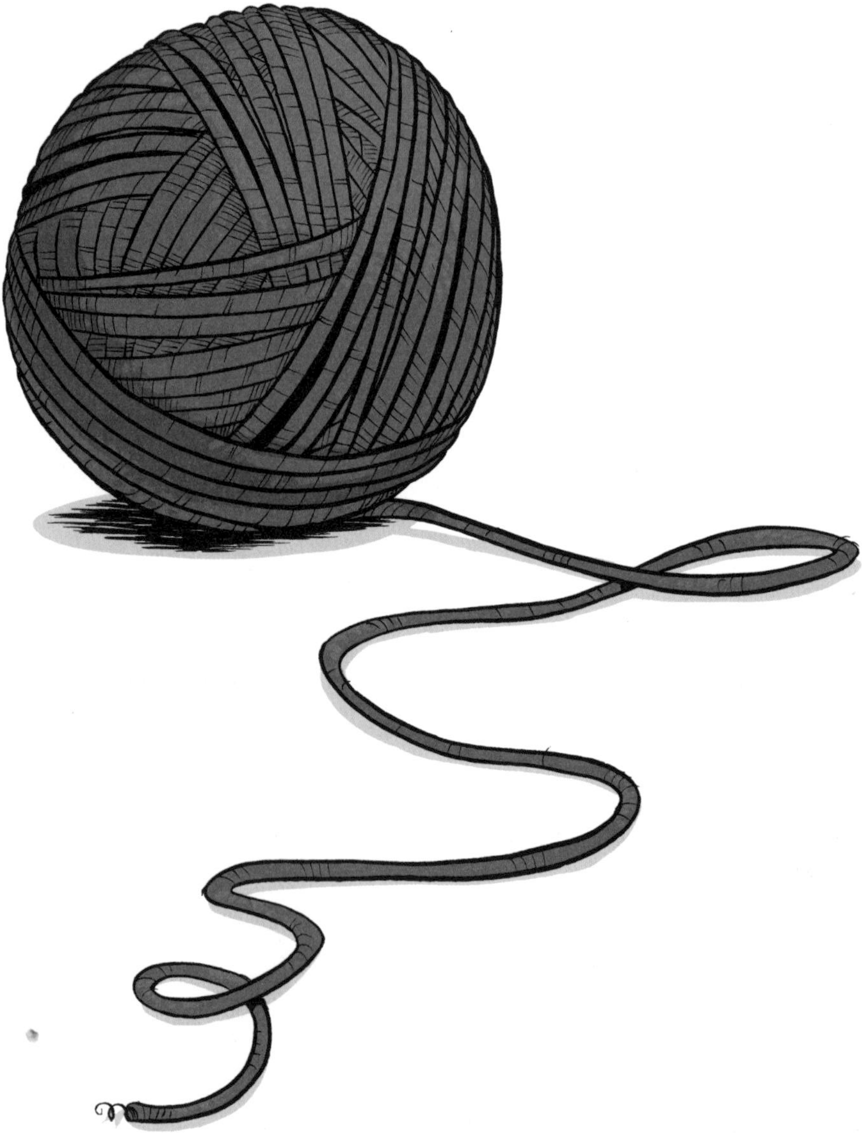

CHAPTER 7

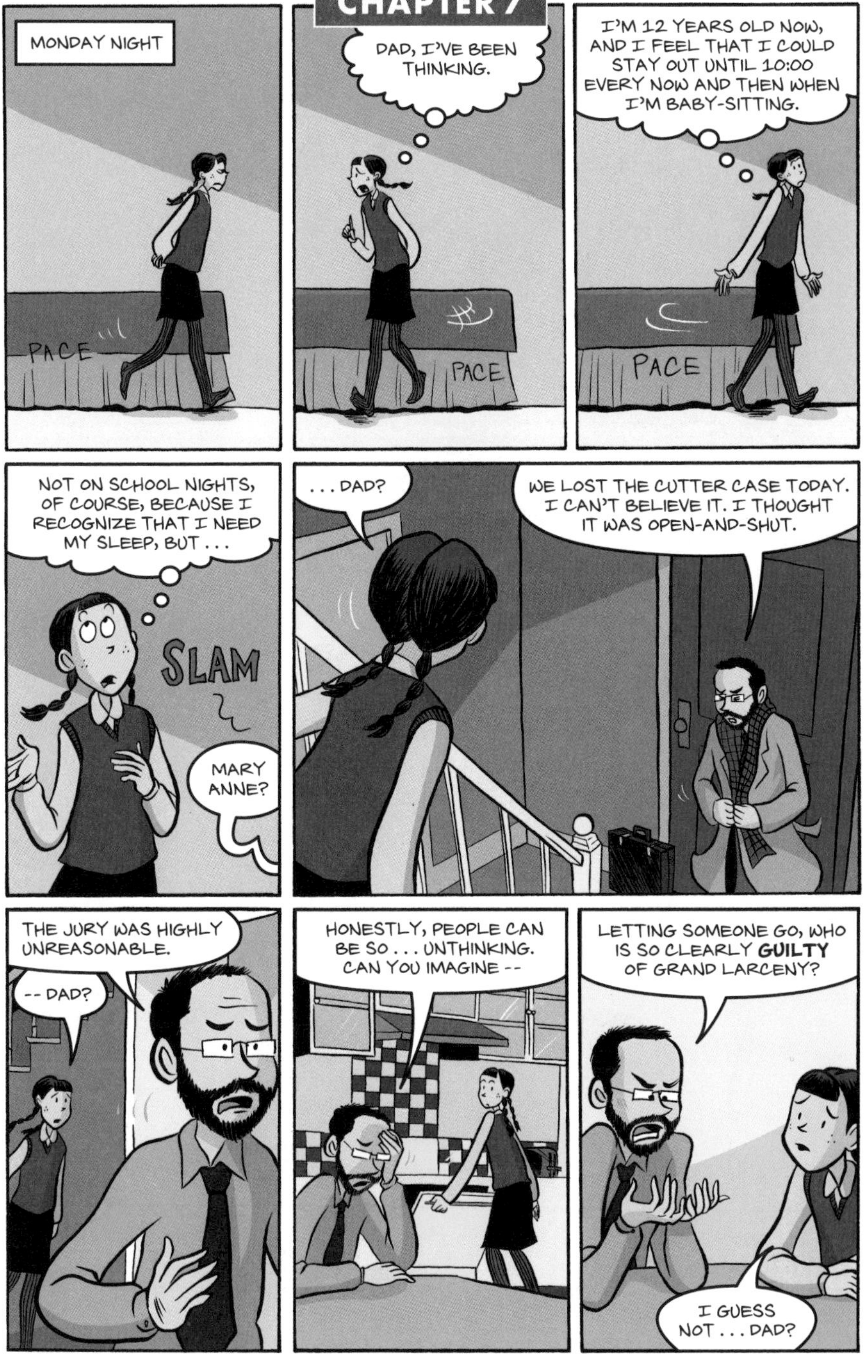
MONDAY NIGHT
DAD, I'VE BEEN THINKING.
PACE
I'M 12 YEARS OLD NOW, AND I FEEL THAT I COULD STAY OUT UNTIL 10:00 EVERY NOW AND THEN WHEN I'M BABY-SITTING.
PACE
PACE
NOT ON SCHOOL NIGHTS, OF COURSE, BECAUSE I RECOGNIZE THAT I NEED MY SLEEP, BUT . . .
SLAM
MARY ANNE?
. . . DAD?
WE LOST THE CUTTER CASE TODAY. I CAN'T BELIEVE IT. I THOUGHT IT WAS OPEN-AND-SHUT.
THE JURY WAS HIGHLY UNREASONABLE.
-- DAD?
HONESTLY, PEOPLE CAN BE SO . . . UNTHINKING. CAN YOU IMAGINE --
LETTING SOMEONE GO, WHO IS SO CLEARLY **GUILTY** OF GRAND LARCENY?
I GUESS NOT . . . DAD?

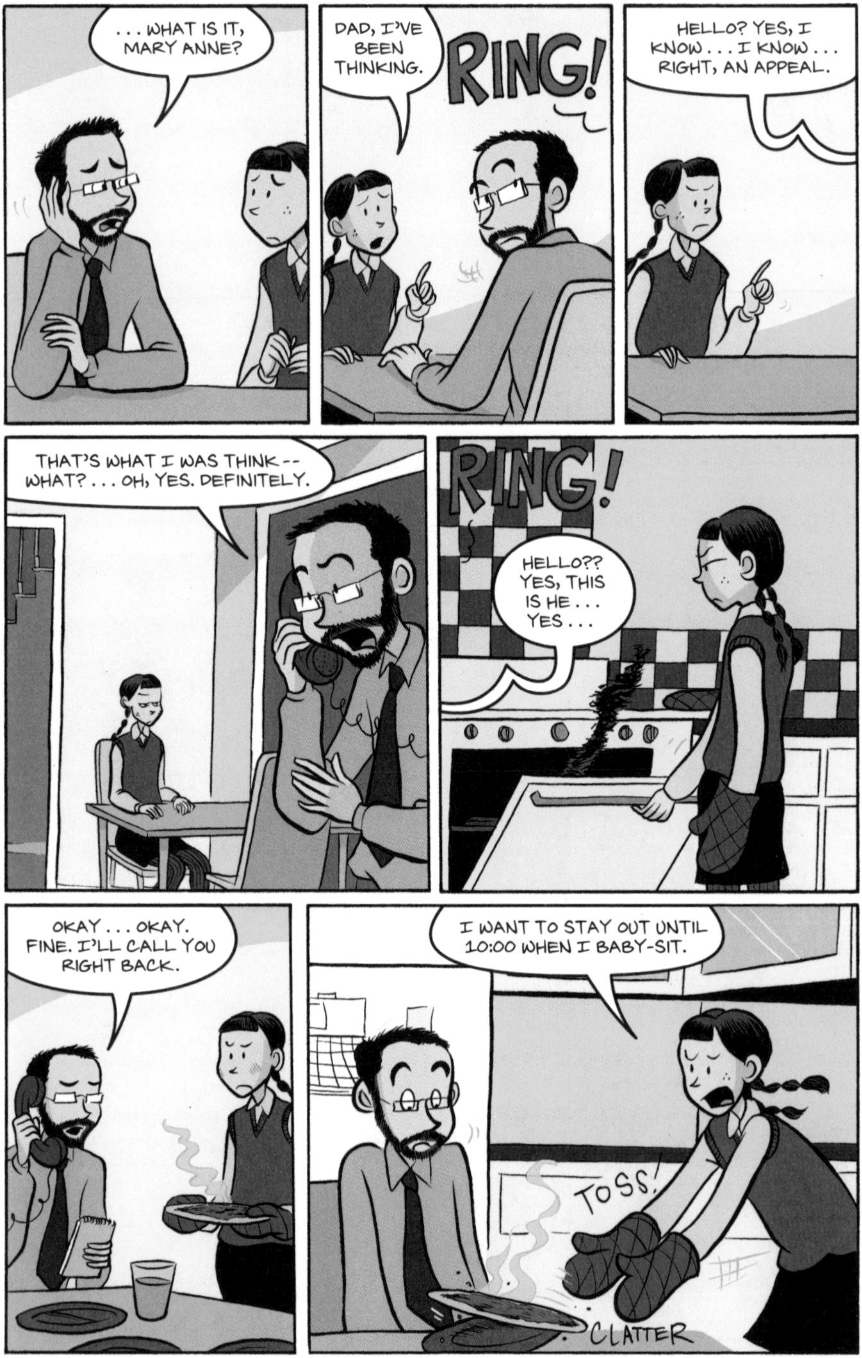
. . . WHAT IS IT, MARY ANNE?
DAD, I'VE BEEN THINKING.
RING!
HELLO? YES, I KNOW . . . I KNOW . . . RIGHT, AN APPEAL.
THAT'S WHAT I WAS THINK -- WHAT? . . . OH, YES. DEFINITELY.
RING!
HELLO?? YES, THIS IS HE . . . YES . . .
OKAY . . . OKAY. FINE. I'LL CALL YOU RIGHT BACK.
I WANT TO STAY OUT UNTIL 10:00 WHEN I BABY-SIT.
TOSS!
CLATTER

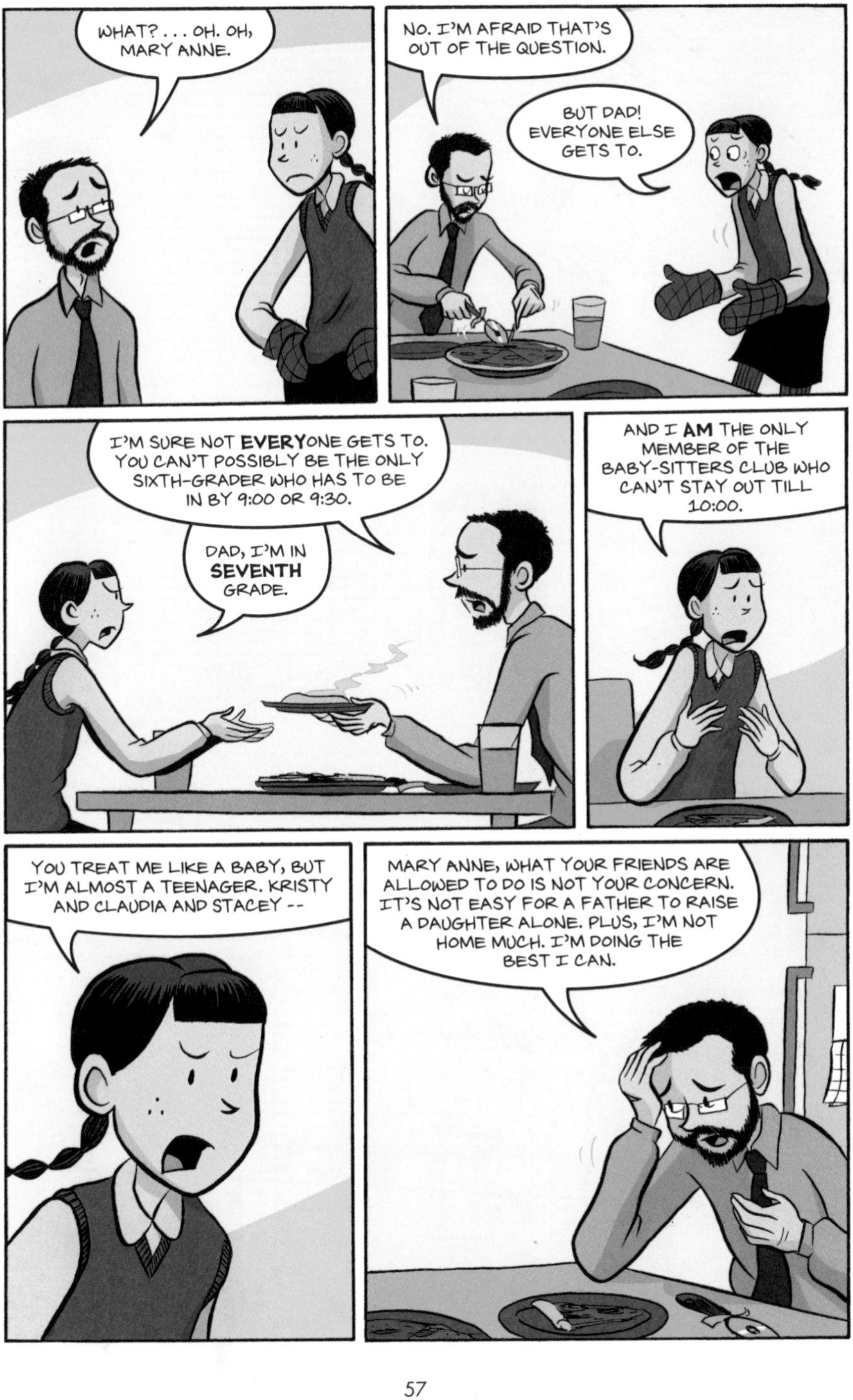
WHAT? . . . OH. OH, MARY ANNE.
NO. I'M AFRAID THAT'S OUT OF THE QUESTION.
BUT DAD! EVERYONE ELSE GETS TO.
I'M SURE NOT **EVERY**ONE GETS TO. YOU CAN'T POSSIBLY BE THE ONLY SIXTH-GRADER WHO HAS TO BE IN BY 9:00 OR 9:30.
DAD, I'M IN **SEVENTH** GRADE.
AND I **AM** THE ONLY MEMBER OF THE BABY-SITTERS CLUB WHO CAN'T STAY OUT TILL 10:00.
YOU TREAT ME LIKE A BABY, BUT I'M ALMOST A TEENAGER. KRISTY AND CLAUDIA AND STACEY --
MARY ANNE, WHAT YOUR FRIENDS ARE ALLOWED TO DO IS NOT YOUR CONCERN. IT'S NOT EASY FOR A FATHER TO RAISE A DAUGHTER ALONE. PLUS, I'M NOT HOME MUCH. I'M DOING THE BEST I CAN.

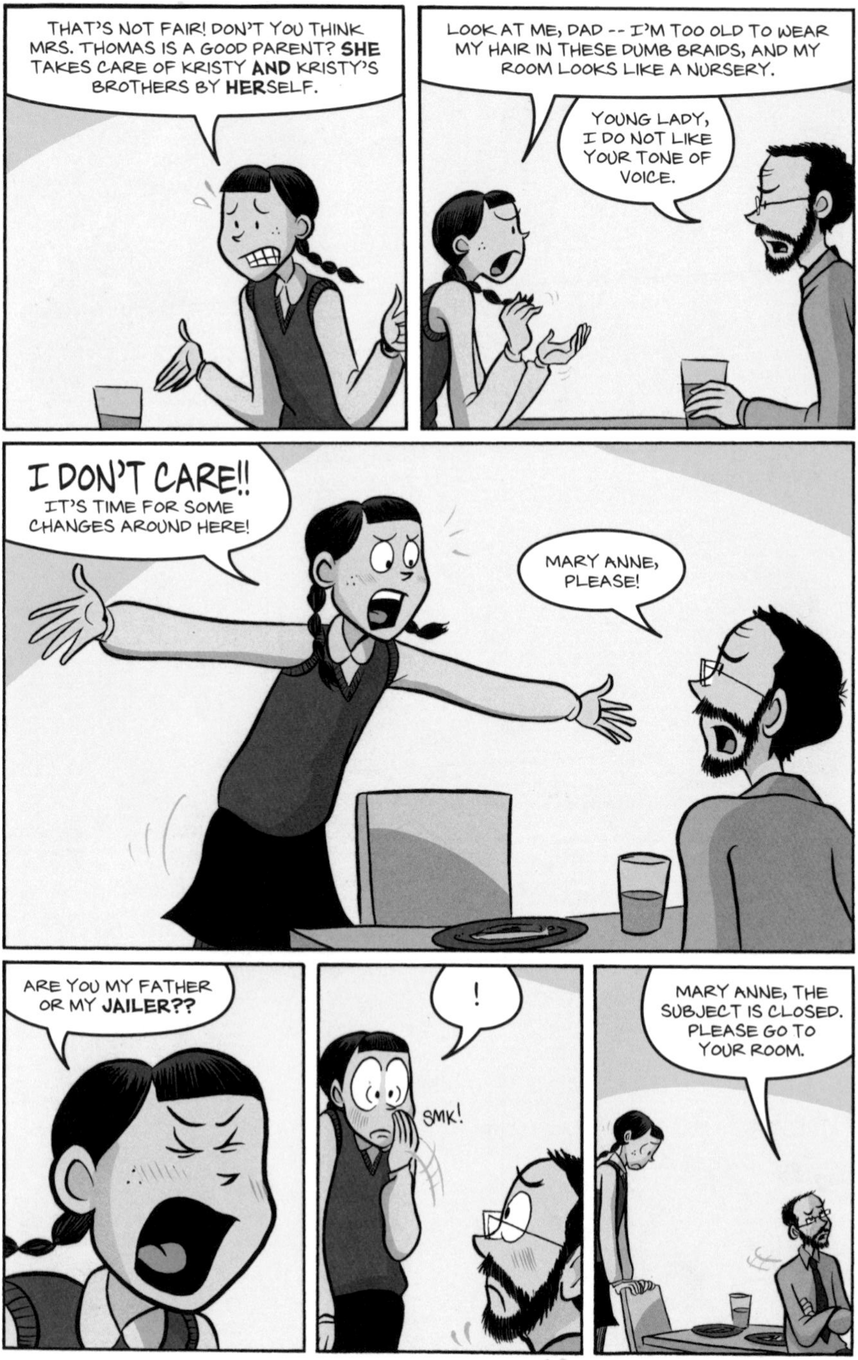
THAT'S NOT FAIR! DON'T YOU THINK MRS. THOMAS IS A GOOD PARENT? SHE TAKES CARE OF KRISTY AND KRISTY'S BROTHERS BY HERSELF.
LOOK AT ME, DAD -- I'M TOO OLD TO WEAR MY HAIR IN THESE DUMB BRAIDS, AND MY ROOM LOOKS LIKE A NURSERY.
YOUNG LADY, I DO NOT LIKE YOUR TONE OF VOICE.
I DON'T CARE!! IT'S TIME FOR SOME CHANGES AROUND HERE!
MARY ANNE, PLEASE!
ARE YOU MY FATHER OR MY JAILER??
!
SMK!
MARY ANNE, THE SUBJECT IS CLOSED. PLEASE GO TO YOUR ROOM.

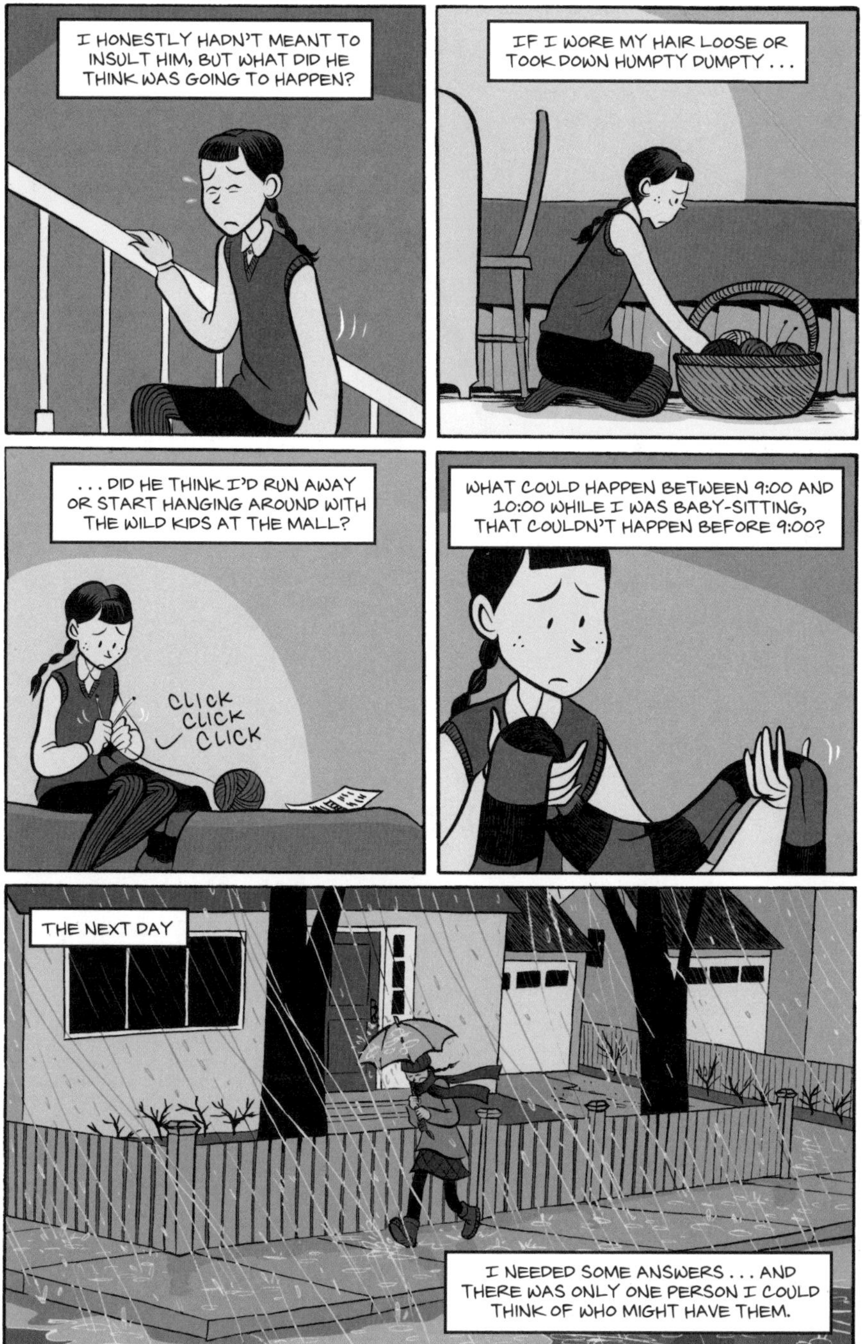
I HONESTLY HADN'T MEANT TO INSULT HIM, BUT WHAT DID HE THINK WAS GOING TO HAPPEN?
IF I WORE MY HAIR LOOSE OR TOOK DOWN HUMPTY DUMPTY . . .
. . . DID HE THINK I'D RUN AWAY OR START HANGING AROUND WITH THE WILD KIDS AT THE MALL?
CLICK CLICK CLICK
WHAT COULD HAPPEN BETWEEN 9:00 AND 10:00 WHILE I WAS BABY-SITTING, THAT COULDN'T HAPPEN BEFORE 9:00?
THE NEXT DAY
I NEEDED SOME ANSWERS . . . AND THERE WAS ONLY ONE PERSON I COULD THINK OF WHO MIGHT HAVE THEM.

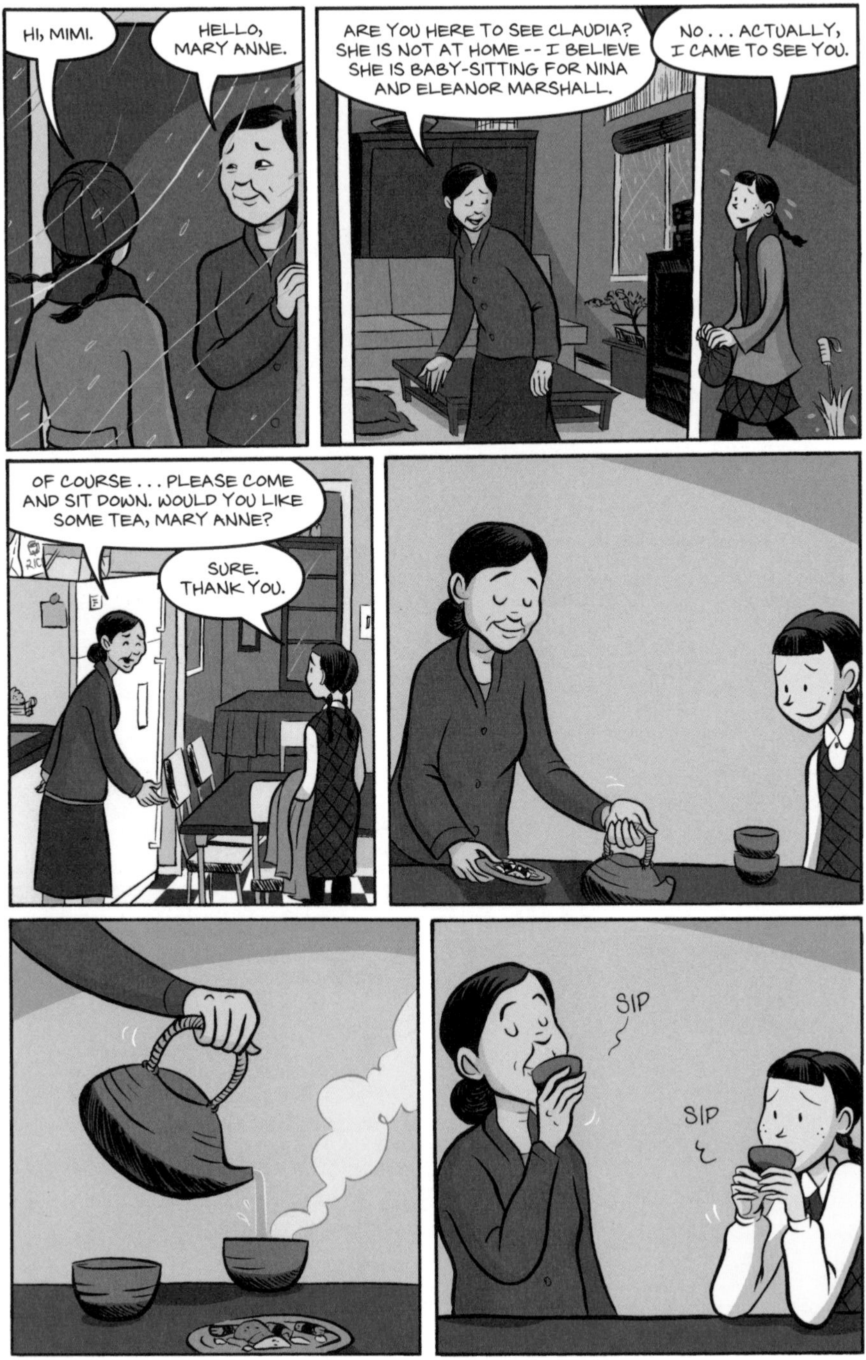
HI, MIMI.
HELLO, MARY ANNE.
ARE YOU HERE TO SEE CLAUDIA? SHE IS NOT AT HOME -- I BELIEVE SHE IS BABY-SITTING FOR NINA AND ELEANOR MARSHALL.
NO . . . ACTUALLY, I CAME TO SEE YOU.
OF COURSE . . . PLEASE COME AND SIT DOWN. WOULD YOU LIKE SOME TEA, MARY ANNE?
SURE. THANK YOU.
SIP
SIP

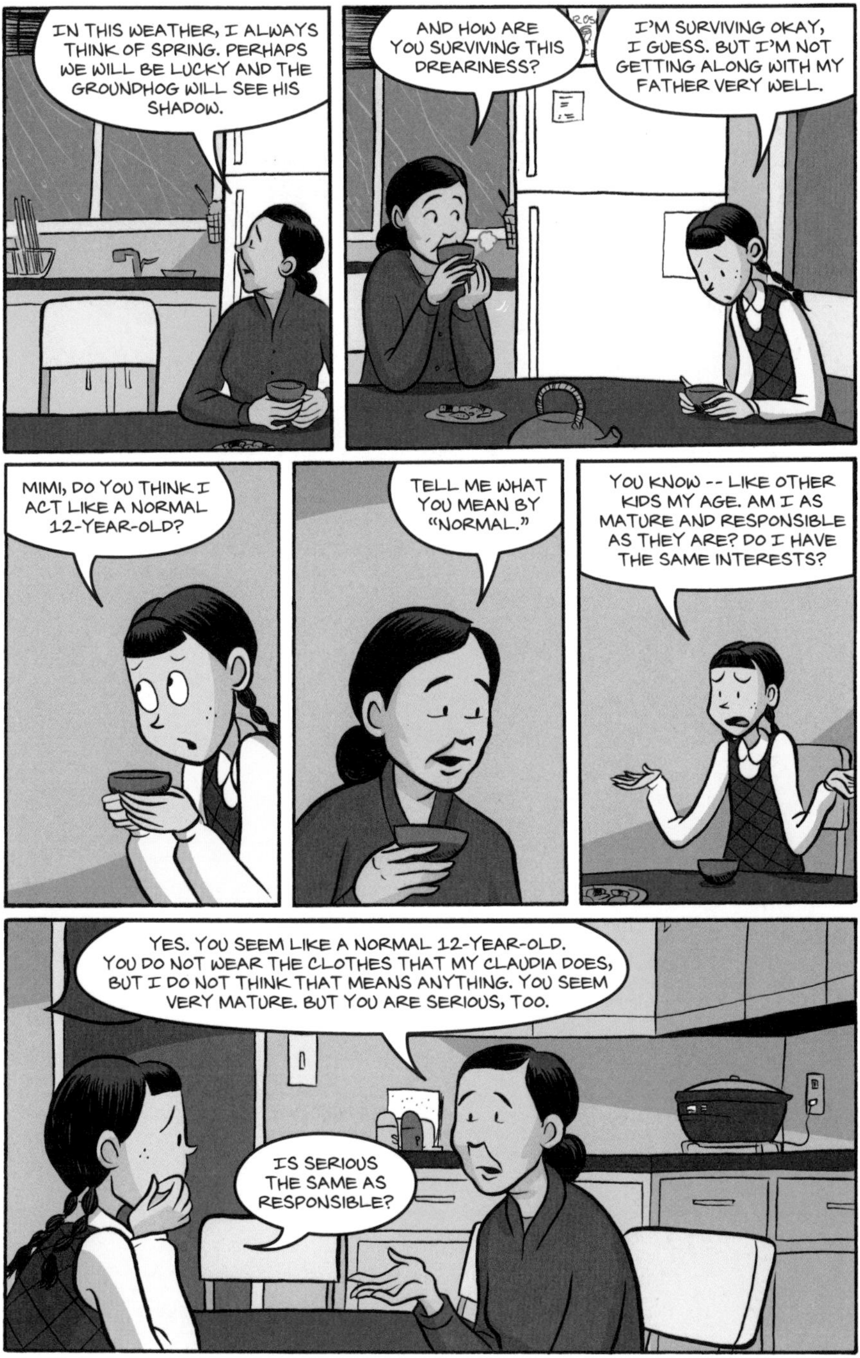
IN THIS WEATHER, I ALWAYS THINK OF SPRING. PERHAPS WE WILL BE LUCKY AND THE GROUNDHOG WILL SEE HIS SHADOW.
AND HOW ARE YOU SURVIVING THIS DREARINESS?
I'M SURVIVING OKAY, I GUESS. BUT I'M NOT GETTING ALONG WITH MY FATHER VERY WELL.
MIMI, DO YOU THINK I ACT LIKE A NORMAL 12-YEAR-OLD?
TELL ME WHAT YOU MEAN BY "NORMAL."
YOU KNOW -- LIKE OTHER KIDS MY AGE. AM I AS MATURE AND RESPONSIBLE AS THEY ARE? DO I HAVE THE SAME INTERESTS?
YES. YOU SEEM LIKE A NORMAL 12-YEAR-OLD. YOU DO NOT WEAR THE CLOTHES THAT MY CLAUDIA DOES, BUT I DO NOT THINK THAT MEANS ANYTHING. YOU SEEM VERY MATURE. BUT YOU ARE SERIOUS, TOO.
IS SERIOUS THE SAME AS RESPONSIBLE?

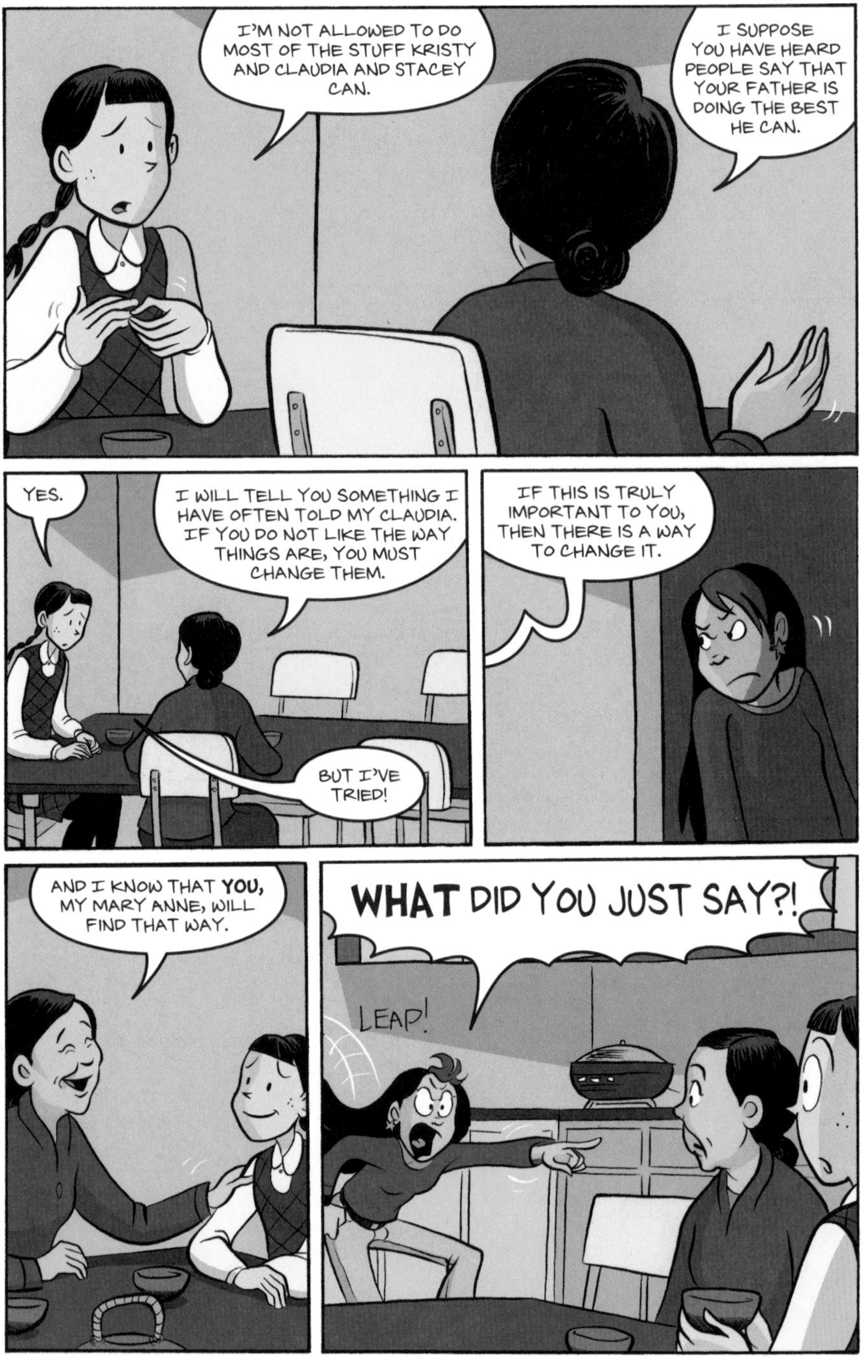
I'M NOT ALLOWED TO DO MOST OF THE STUFF KRISTY AND CLAUDIA AND STACEY CAN.
I SUPPOSE YOU HAVE HEARD PEOPLE SAY THAT YOUR FATHER IS DOING THE BEST HE CAN.
YES.
I WILL TELL YOU SOMETHING I HAVE OFTEN TOLD MY CLAUDIA. IF YOU DO NOT LIKE THE WAY THINGS ARE, YOU MUST CHANGE THEM.
BUT I'VE TRIED!
IF THIS IS TRULY IMPORTANT TO YOU, THEN THERE IS A WAY TO CHANGE IT.
AND I KNOW THAT **YOU**, MY MARY ANNE, WILL FIND THAT WAY.
WHAT DID YOU JUST SAY?!
LEAP!

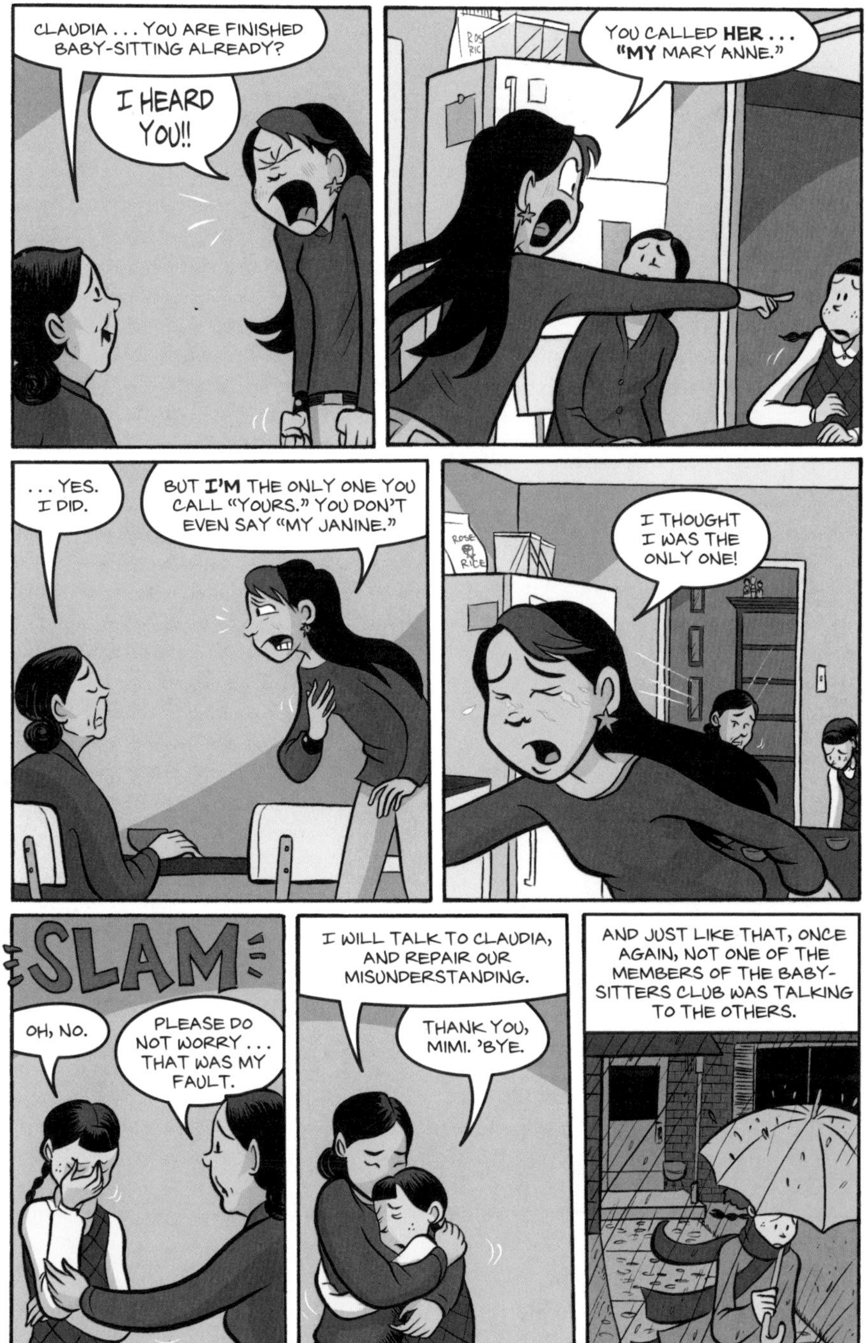
CLAUDIA . . . YOU ARE FINISHED BABY-SITTING ALREADY?
I HEARD YOU!!
YOU CALLED **HER . . .** "**MY** MARY ANNE."
. . . YES. I DID.
BUT **I'M** THE ONLY ONE YOU CALL "YOURS." YOU DON'T EVEN SAY "MY JANINE."
I THOUGHT I WAS THE ONLY ONE!
SLAM
OH, NO.
PLEASE DO NOT WORRY . . . THAT WAS MY FAULT.
I WILL TALK TO CLAUDIA, AND REPAIR OUR MISUNDERSTANDING.
THANK YOU, MIMI. 'BYE.
AND JUST LIKE THAT, ONCE AGAIN, NOT ONE OF THE MEMBERS OF THE BABY-SITTERS CLUB WAS TALKING TO THE OTHERS.

Teusday, Januay 20

I am so made! I know this notebook is
for writing our siting jobs so we can keep
track of club problems. Well, this is not
a sitting job, but I have a club probleme.
Her name is Mary Anne Spier or as she
is otherwise known MY MARY ANNE. Where
does Mary Anne get off being so chummy
with Mimi? It isn't fair. It's one thing
for Mimi to help her with her ~~niting~~ knitting
but today they were sharing tea in the
special cups and Mimi called her
My Mary Anne. NO FAIR. So there.
                    * Claudia *

CHAPTER 8

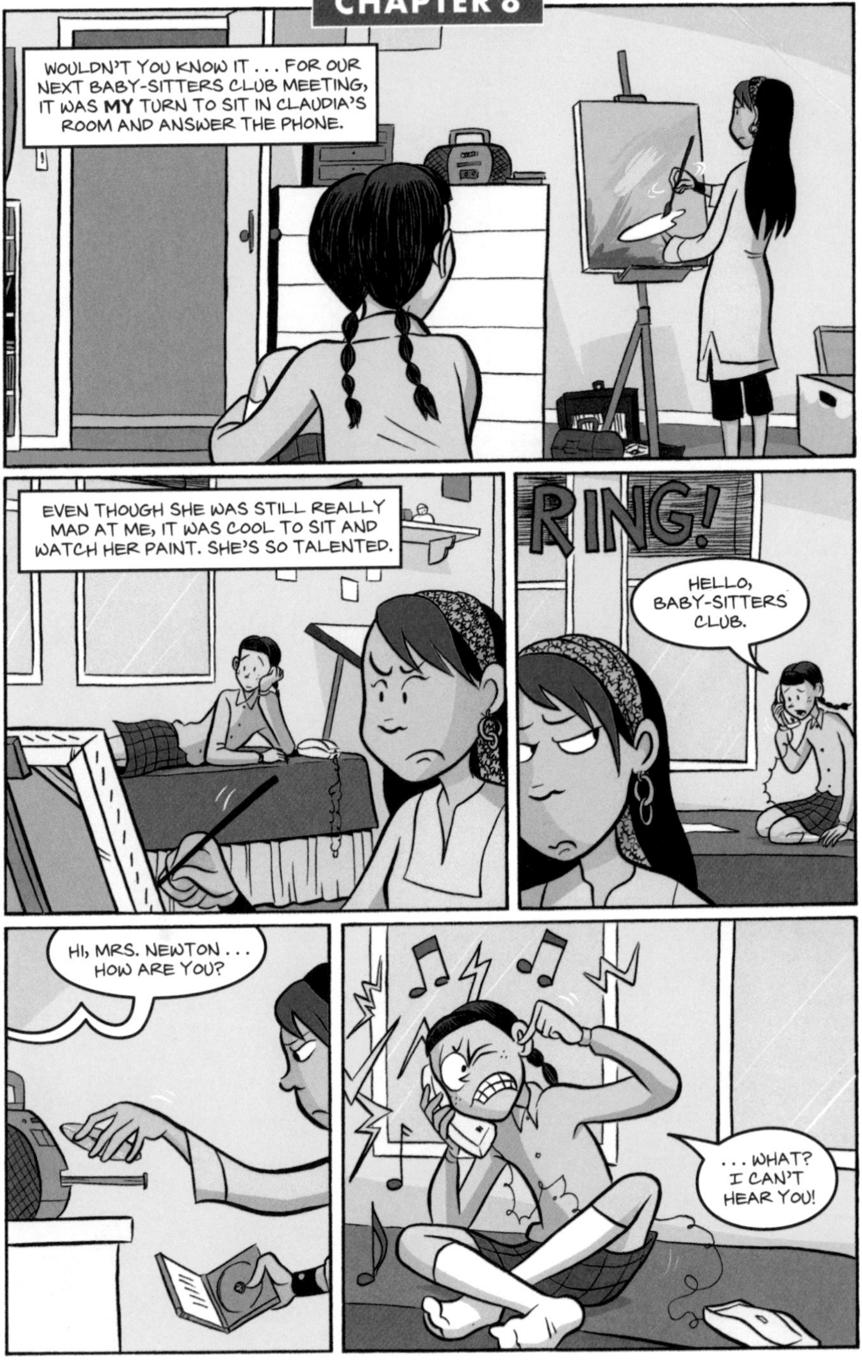

WOULDN'T YOU KNOW IT . . . FOR OUR NEXT BABY-SITTERS CLUB MEETING, IT WAS **MY** TURN TO SIT IN CLAUDIA'S ROOM AND ANSWER THE PHONE.
EVEN THOUGH SHE WAS STILL REALLY MAD AT ME, IT WAS COOL TO SIT AND WATCH HER PAINT. SHE'S SO TALENTED.
RING!
HELLO, BABY-SITTERS CLUB.
HI, MRS. NEWTON . . . HOW ARE YOU?
. . . WHAT? I CAN'T HEAR YOU!

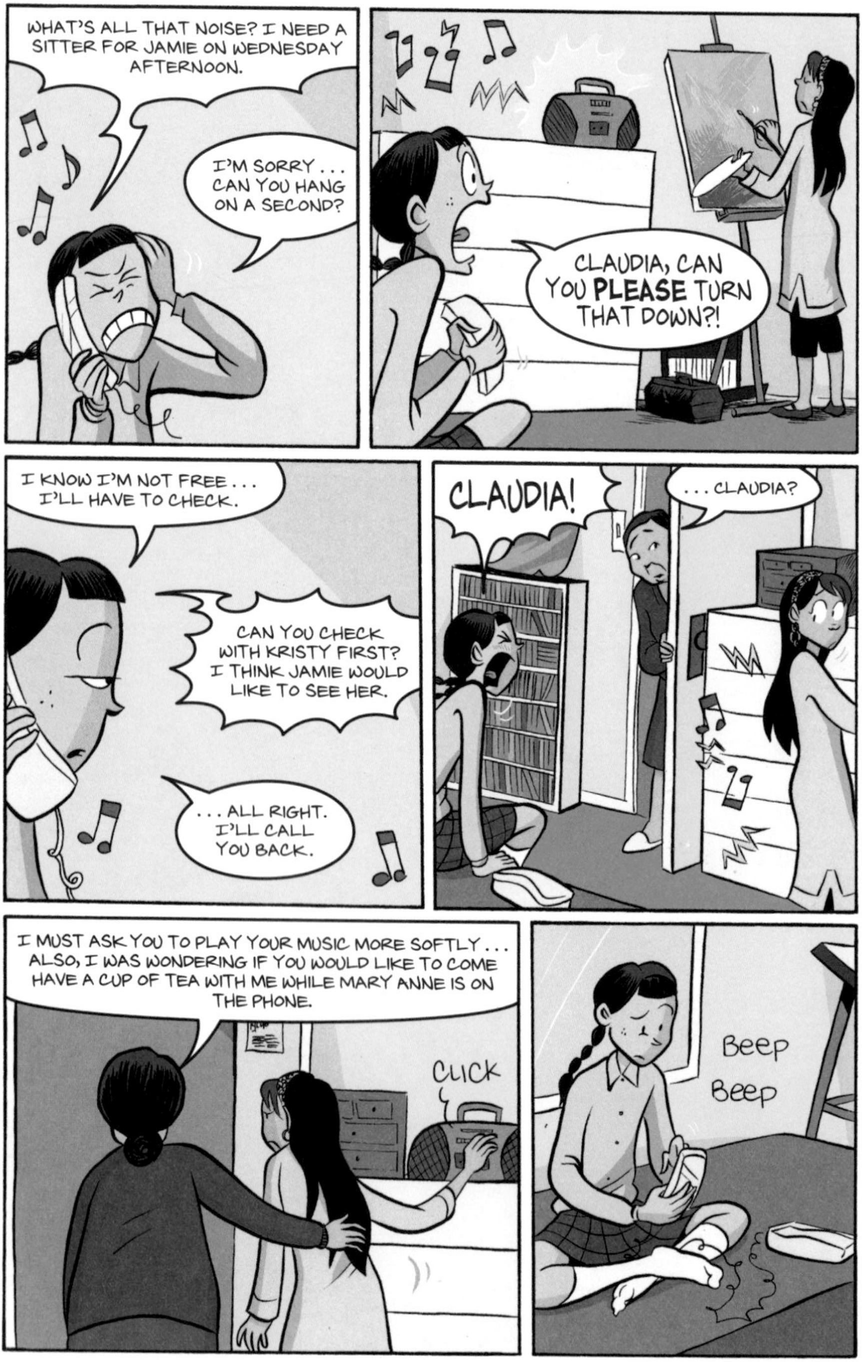
WHAT'S ALL THAT NOISE? I NEED A SITTER FOR JAMIE ON WEDNESDAY AFTERNOON.
I'M SORRY . . . CAN YOU HANG ON A SECOND?
CLAUDIA, CAN YOU **PLEASE** TURN THAT DOWN?!
I KNOW I'M NOT FREE . . . I'LL HAVE TO CHECK.
CAN YOU CHECK WITH KRISTY FIRST? I THINK JAMIE WOULD LIKE TO SEE HER.
. . . ALL RIGHT. I'LL CALL YOU BACK.
CLAUDIA!
. . . CLAUDIA?
I MUST ASK YOU TO PLAY YOUR MUSIC MORE SOFTLY . . . ALSO, I WAS WONDERING IF YOU WOULD LIKE TO COME HAVE A CUP OF TEA WITH ME WHILE MARY ANNE IS ON THE PHONE.
CLICK
Beep
Beep

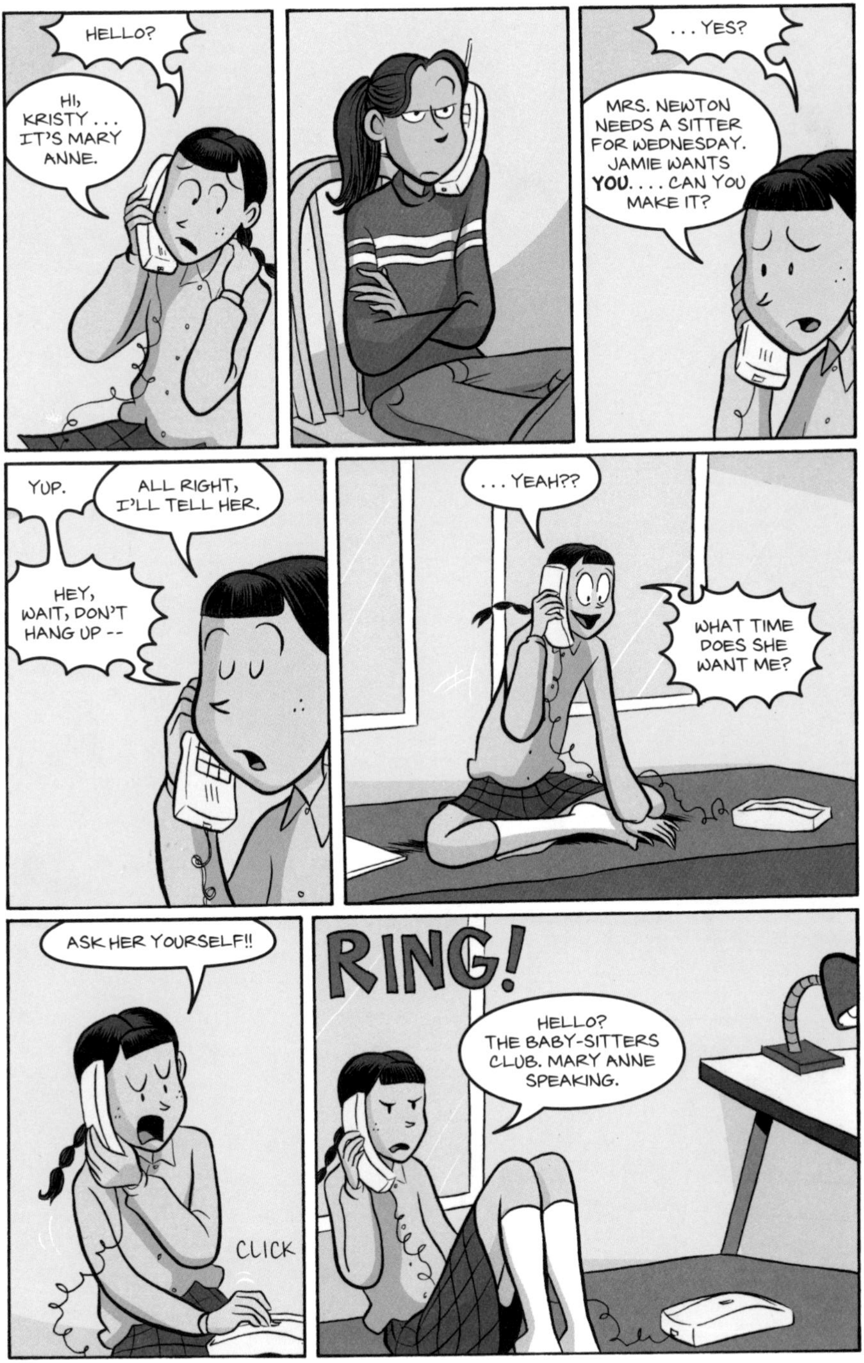

HELLO?
HI, KRISTY . . . IT'S MARY ANNE.
. . . YES?
MRS. NEWTON NEEDS A SITTER FOR WEDNESDAY. JAMIE WANTS **YOU**. . . . CAN YOU MAKE IT?
YUP.
ALL RIGHT, I'LL TELL HER.
HEY, WAIT, DON'T HANG UP --
. . . YEAH??
WHAT TIME DOES SHE WANT ME?
ASK HER YOURSELF!!
CLICK
RING!
HELLO? THE BABY-SITTERS CLUB. MARY ANNE SPEAKING.

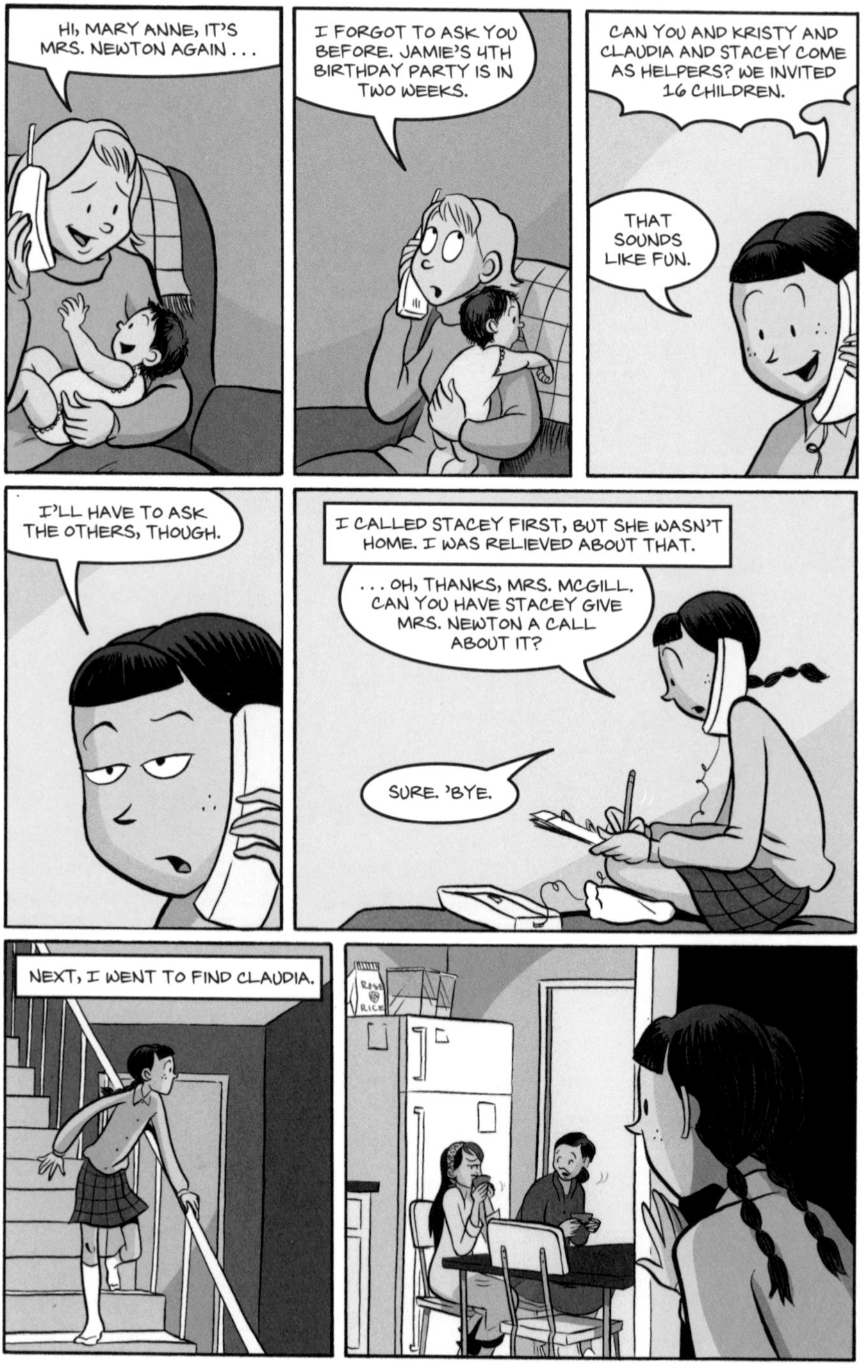
HI, MARY ANNE, IT'S MRS. NEWTON AGAIN . . .
I FORGOT TO ASK YOU BEFORE. JAMIE'S 4TH BIRTHDAY PARTY IS IN TWO WEEKS.
CAN YOU AND KRISTY AND CLAUDIA AND STACEY COME AS HELPERS? WE INVITED 16 CHILDREN.
THAT SOUNDS LIKE FUN.
I'LL HAVE TO ASK THE OTHERS, THOUGH.
I CALLED STACEY FIRST, BUT SHE WASN'T HOME. I WAS RELIEVED ABOUT THAT.
. . . OH, THANKS, MRS. MCGILL. CAN YOU HAVE STACEY GIVE MRS. NEWTON A CALL ABOUT IT?
SURE. 'BYE.
NEXT, I WENT TO FIND CLAUDIA.

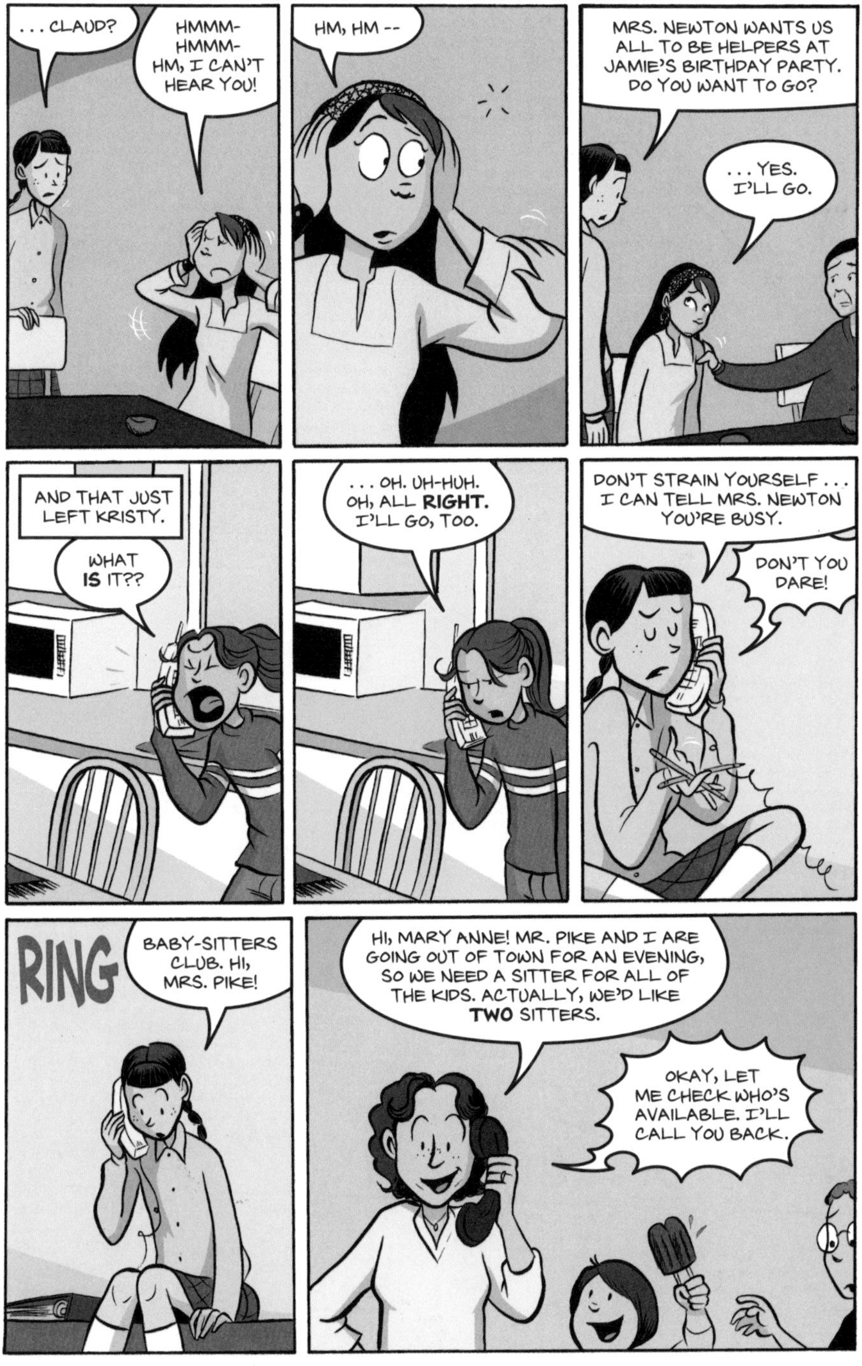
. . . CLAUD?
HMMM-HMMM-HM, I CAN'T HEAR YOU!
HM, HM --
MRS. NEWTON WANTS US ALL TO BE HELPERS AT JAMIE'S BIRTHDAY PARTY. DO YOU WANT TO GO?
. . . YES. I'LL GO.
AND THAT JUST LEFT KRISTY.
WHAT **IS** IT??
. . . OH. UH-HUH. OH, ALL **RIGHT.** I'LL GO, TOO.
DON'T STRAIN YOURSELF . . . I CAN TELL MRS. NEWTON YOU'RE BUSY.
DON'T YOU DARE!
RING
BABY-SITTERS CLUB. HI, MRS. PIKE!
HI, MARY ANNE! MR. PIKE AND I ARE GOING OUT OF TOWN FOR AN EVENING, SO WE NEED A SITTER FOR ALL OF THE KIDS. ACTUALLY, WE'D LIKE **TWO** SITTERS.
OKAY, LET ME CHECK WHO'S AVAILABLE. I'LL CALL YOU BACK.

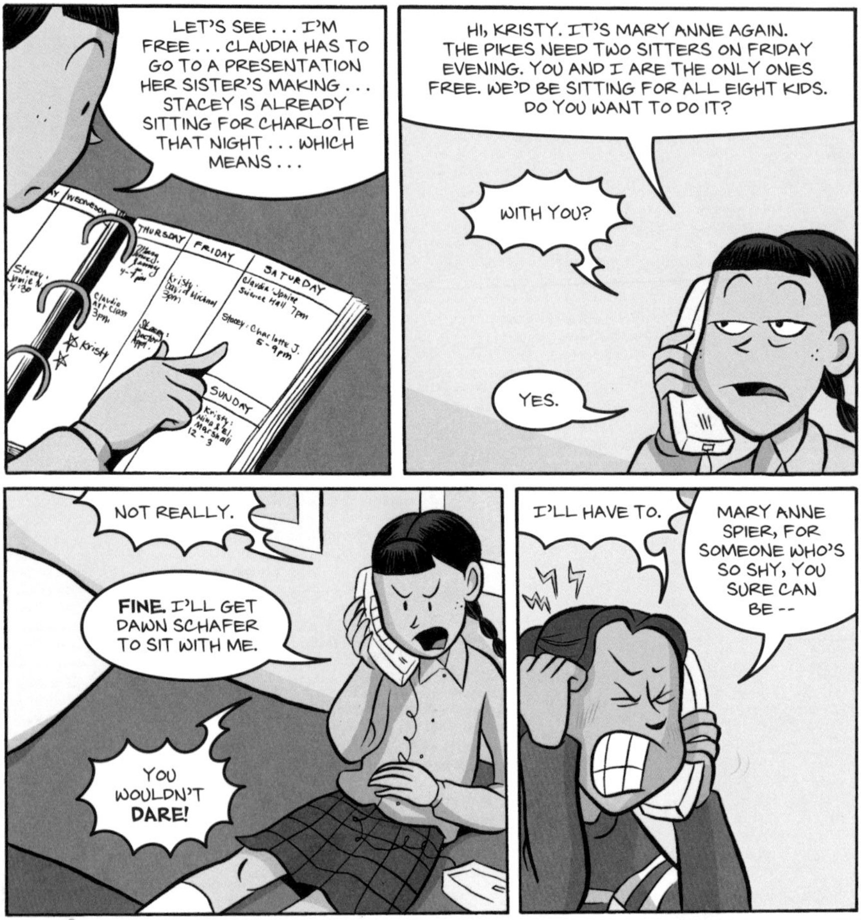
LET'S SEE . . . I'M FREE . . . CLAUDIA HAS TO GO TO A PRESENTATION HER SISTER'S MAKING . . . STACEY IS ALREADY SITTING FOR CHARLOTTE THAT NIGHT . . . WHICH MEANS . . .
THURSDAY
FRIDAY
SATURDAY
SUNDAY
Claudia: Janine Science Hall 7pm
Stacey: Charlotte J. 5-9pm
HI, KRISTY. IT'S MARY ANNE AGAIN. THE PIKES NEED TWO SITTERS ON FRIDAY EVENING. YOU AND I ARE THE ONLY ONES FREE. WE'D BE SITTING FOR ALL EIGHT KIDS. DO YOU WANT TO DO IT?
WITH YOU?
YES.
NOT REALLY.
FINE. I'LL GET DAWN SCHAFER TO SIT WITH ME.
YOU WOULDN'T DARE!
I'LL HAVE TO.
MARY ANNE SPIER, FOR SOMEONE WHO'S SO SHY, YOU SURE CAN BE --
WHAT? WHAT CAN I BE?
NEVER MIND. I'LL SIT WITH YOU.
I WAS NOT LOOKING FORWARD TO BABY-SITTING WITH KRISTIN AMANDA THOMAS.

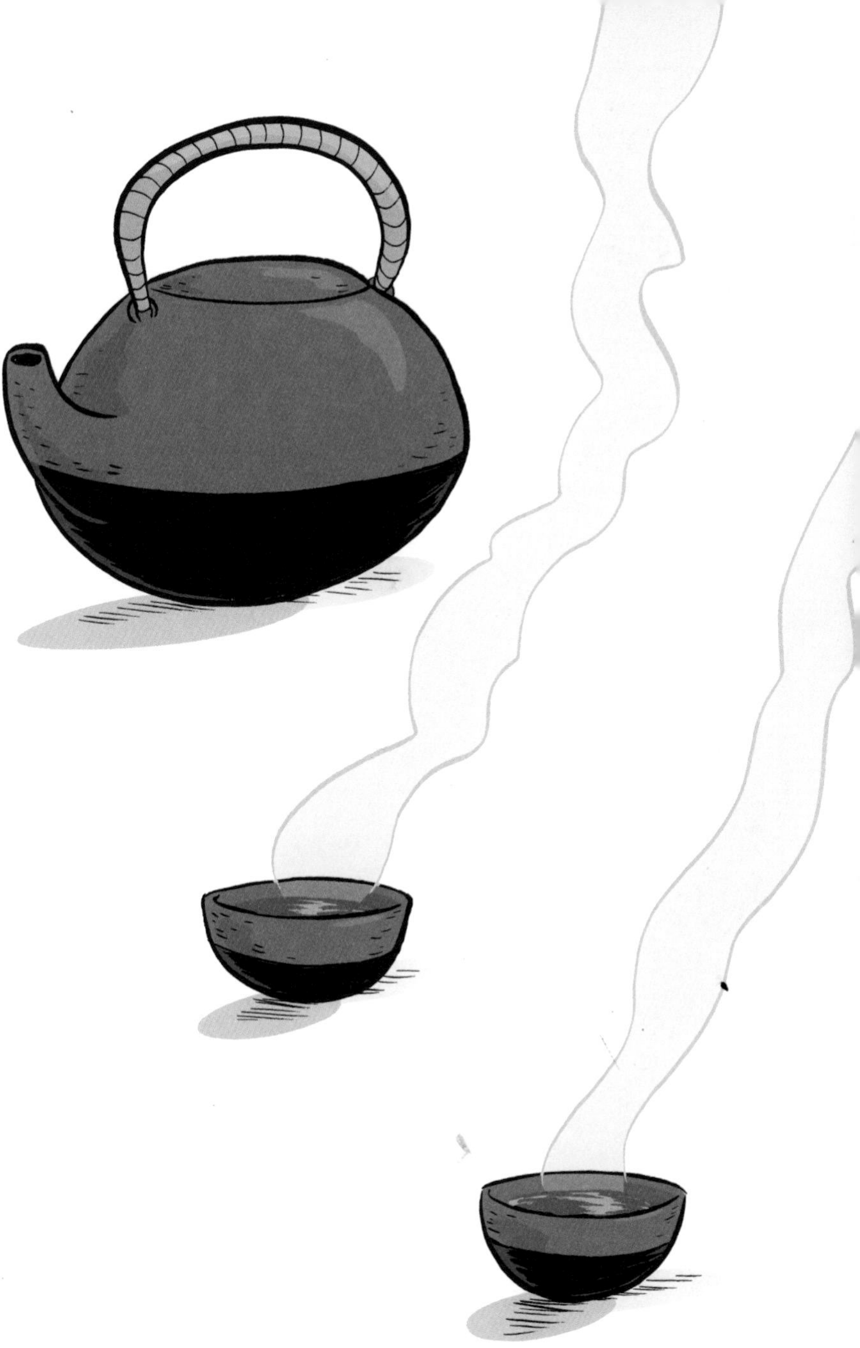

Saturday, January 31

   Yesterday, Mary Anne and I baby-sat for the Pikes. I'm really surprised that we were able to pull it off. Hereby let it be known that it is possible:

1. For two people to baby-sit for eight kids without losing their sanity (the sitters' OR the kids'), and

2. for the baby-sitters to accomplish this without ever speaking to each other.

There should be a Baby-sitters' Hall of Fame where experiences like ours could be recorded and preserved for all to read about. To do what we did takes a lot of imagination.

. . . And a really good fight, I guess.

                                    — Kristy

CHAPTER 9

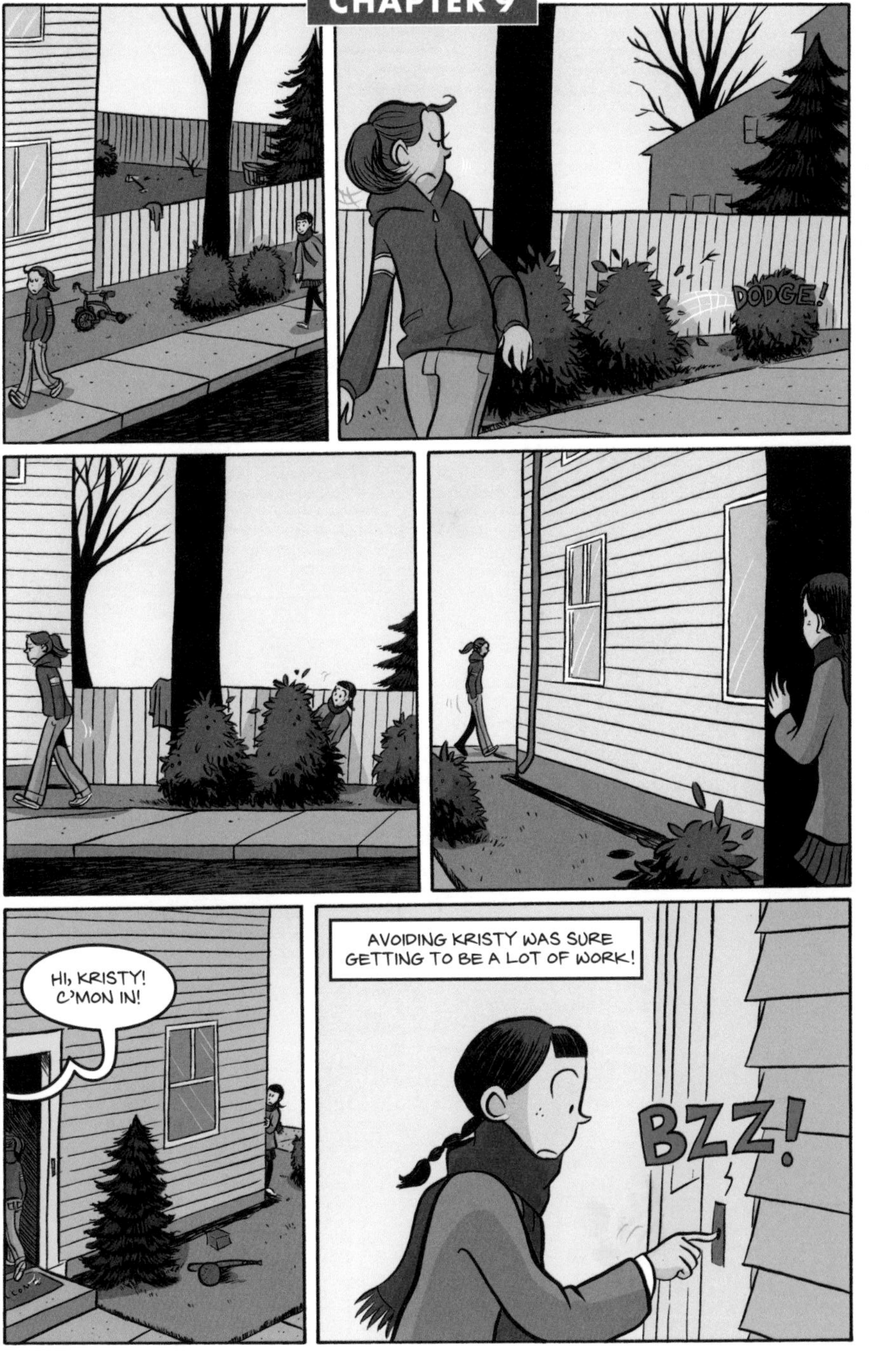
DODGE!
HI, KRISTY! C'MON IN!
AVOIDING KRISTY WAS SURE GETTING TO BE A LOT OF WORK!
BZZ!

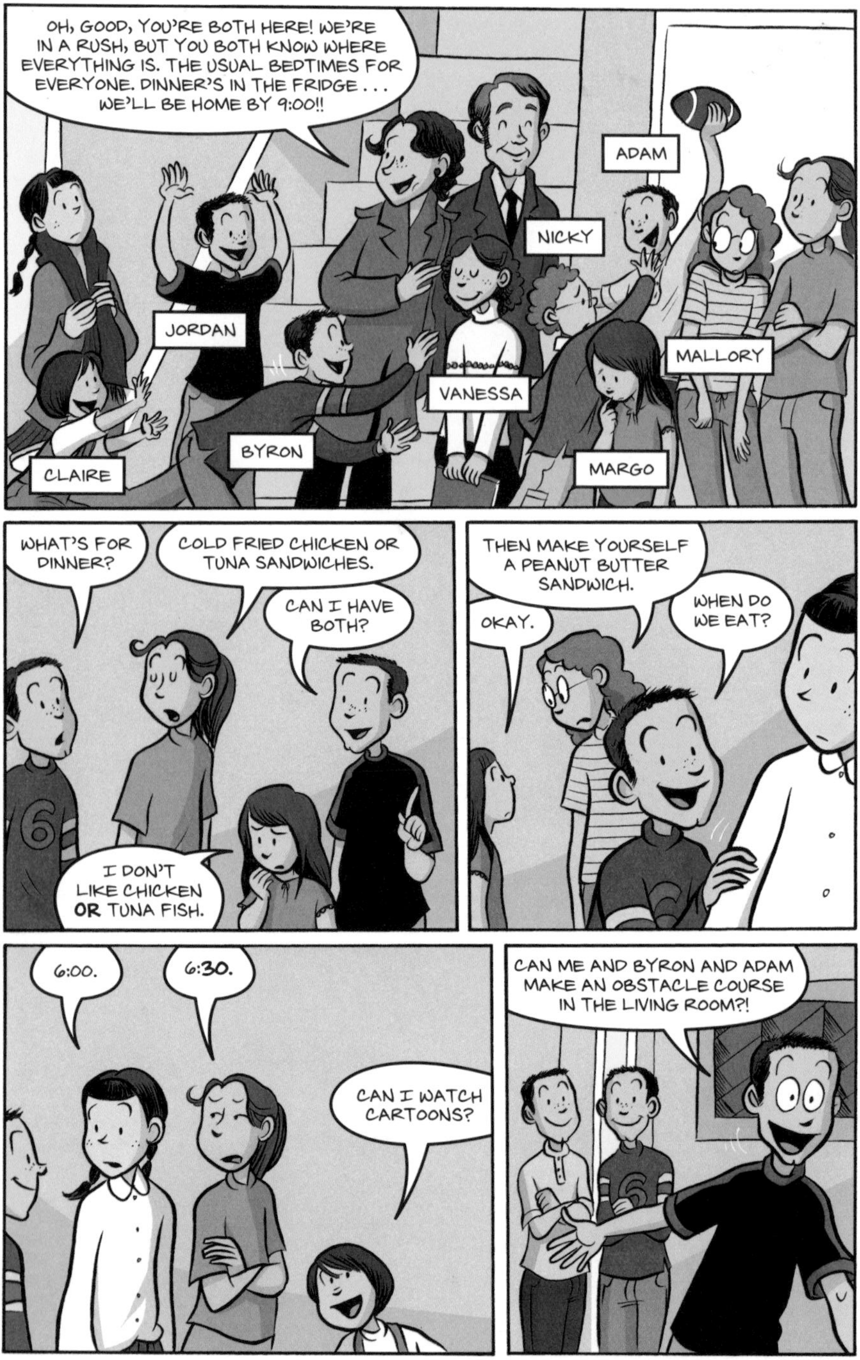
OH, GOOD, YOU'RE BOTH HERE! WE'RE IN A RUSH, BUT YOU BOTH KNOW WHERE EVERYTHING IS. THE USUAL BEDTIMES FOR EVERYONE. DINNER'S IN THE FRIDGE . . . WE'LL BE HOME BY 9:00!!
ADAM
NICKY
JORDAN
MALLORY
VANESSA
BYRON
MARGO
CLAIRE
WHAT'S FOR DINNER?
COLD FRIED CHICKEN OR TUNA SANDWICHES.
CAN I HAVE BOTH?
I DON'T LIKE CHICKEN **OR** TUNA FISH.
THEN MAKE YOURSELF A PEANUT BUTTER SANDWICH.
OKAY.
WHEN DO WE EAT?
6:00.
6:**30**.
CAN I WATCH CARTOONS?
CAN ME AND BYRON AND ADAM MAKE AN OBSTACLE COURSE IN THE LIVING ROOM?!

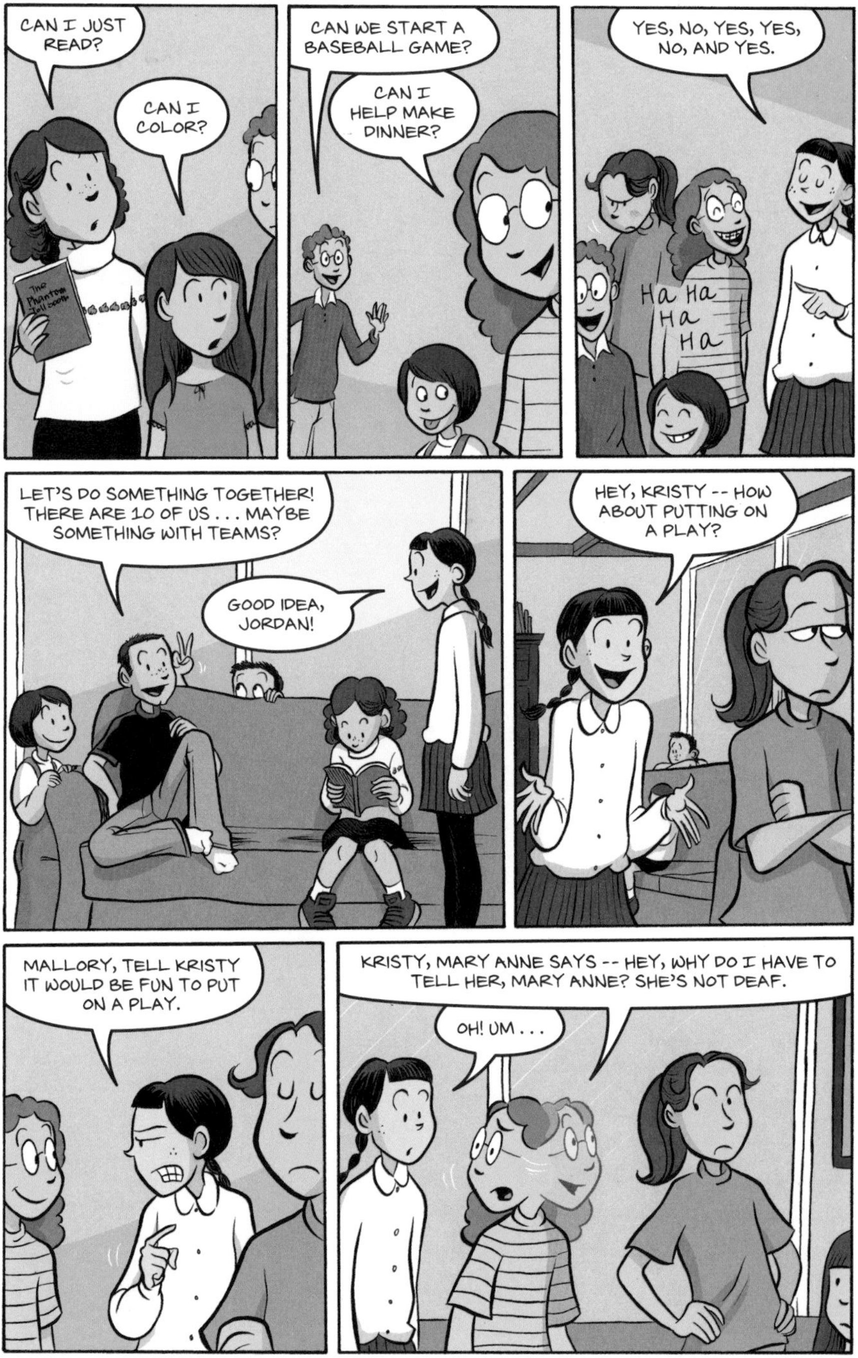
CAN I JUST READ?
CAN I COLOR?
The Phantom Tollbooth
CAN WE START A BASEBALL GAME?
CAN I HELP MAKE DINNER?
YES, NO, YES, YES, NO, AND YES.
Ha Ha Ha Ha
LET'S DO SOMETHING TOGETHER! THERE ARE 10 OF US . . . MAYBE SOMETHING WITH TEAMS?
GOOD IDEA, JORDAN!
HEY, KRISTY -- HOW ABOUT PUTTING ON A PLAY?
MALLORY, TELL KRISTY IT WOULD BE FUN TO PUT ON A PLAY.
KRISTY, MARY ANNE SAYS -- HEY, WHY DO I HAVE TO TELL HER, MARY ANNE? SHE'S NOT DEAF.
OH! UM . . .

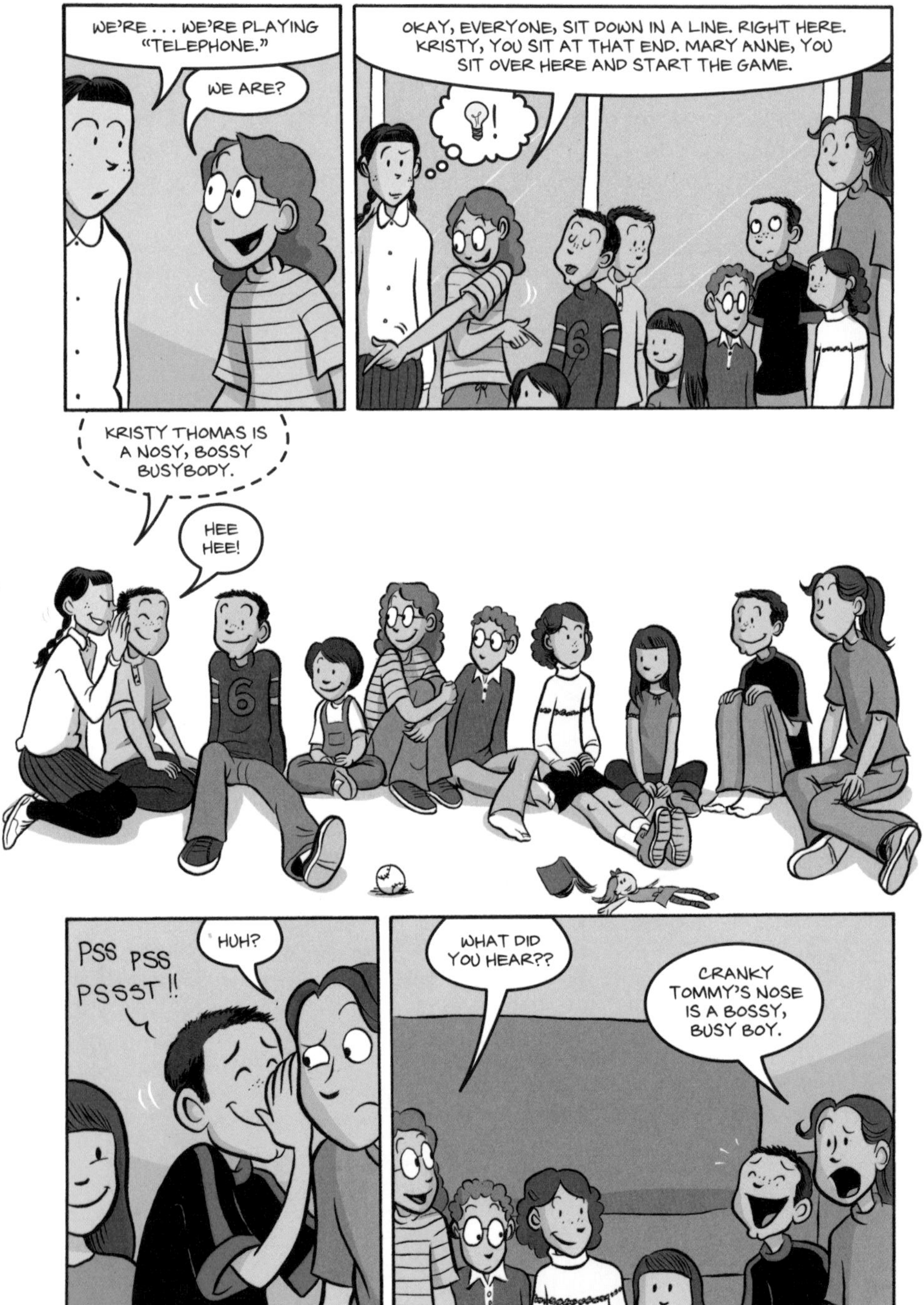
WE'RE . . . WE'RE PLAYING "TELEPHONE."
WE ARE?
OKAY, EVERYONE, SIT DOWN IN A LINE. RIGHT HERE. KRISTY, YOU SIT AT THAT END. MARY ANNE, YOU SIT OVER HERE AND START THE GAME.
!
KRISTY THOMAS IS A NOSY, BOSSY BUSYBODY.
HEE HEE!
PSS PSS PSSST !!
HUH?
WHAT DID YOU HEAR??
CRANKY TOMMY'S NOSE IS A BOSSY, BUSY BOY.

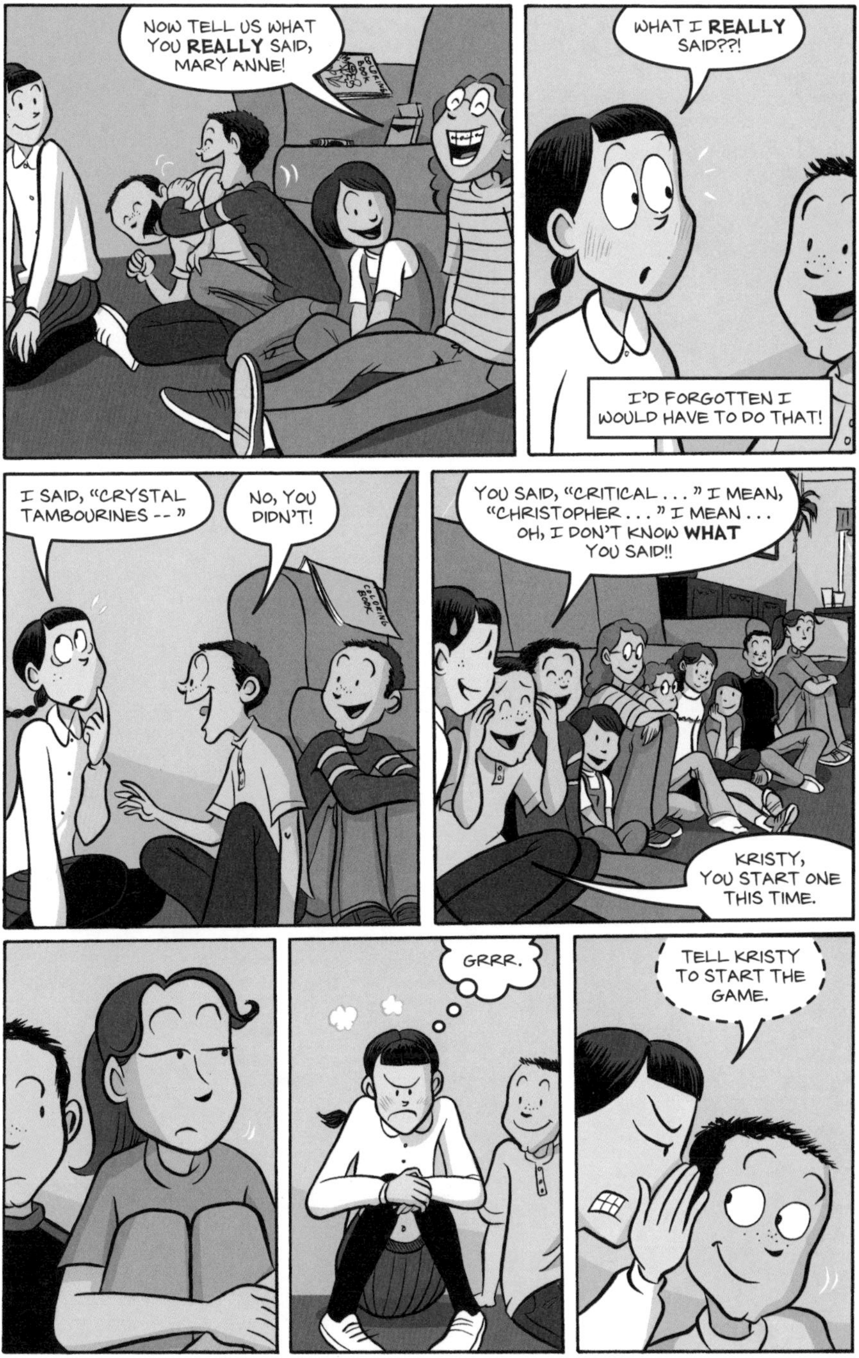
NOW TELL US WHAT YOU **REALLY** SAID, MARY ANNE!
WHAT I **REALLY** SAID??!
I'D FORGOTTEN I WOULD HAVE TO DO THAT!
I SAID, "CRYSTAL TAMBOURINES --"
NO, YOU DIDN'T!
YOU SAID, "CRITICAL . . ." I MEAN, "CHRISTOPHER . . ." I MEAN . . . OH, I DON'T KNOW **WHAT** YOU SAID!!
KRISTY, YOU START ONE THIS TIME.
GRRR.
TELL KRISTY TO START THE GAME.

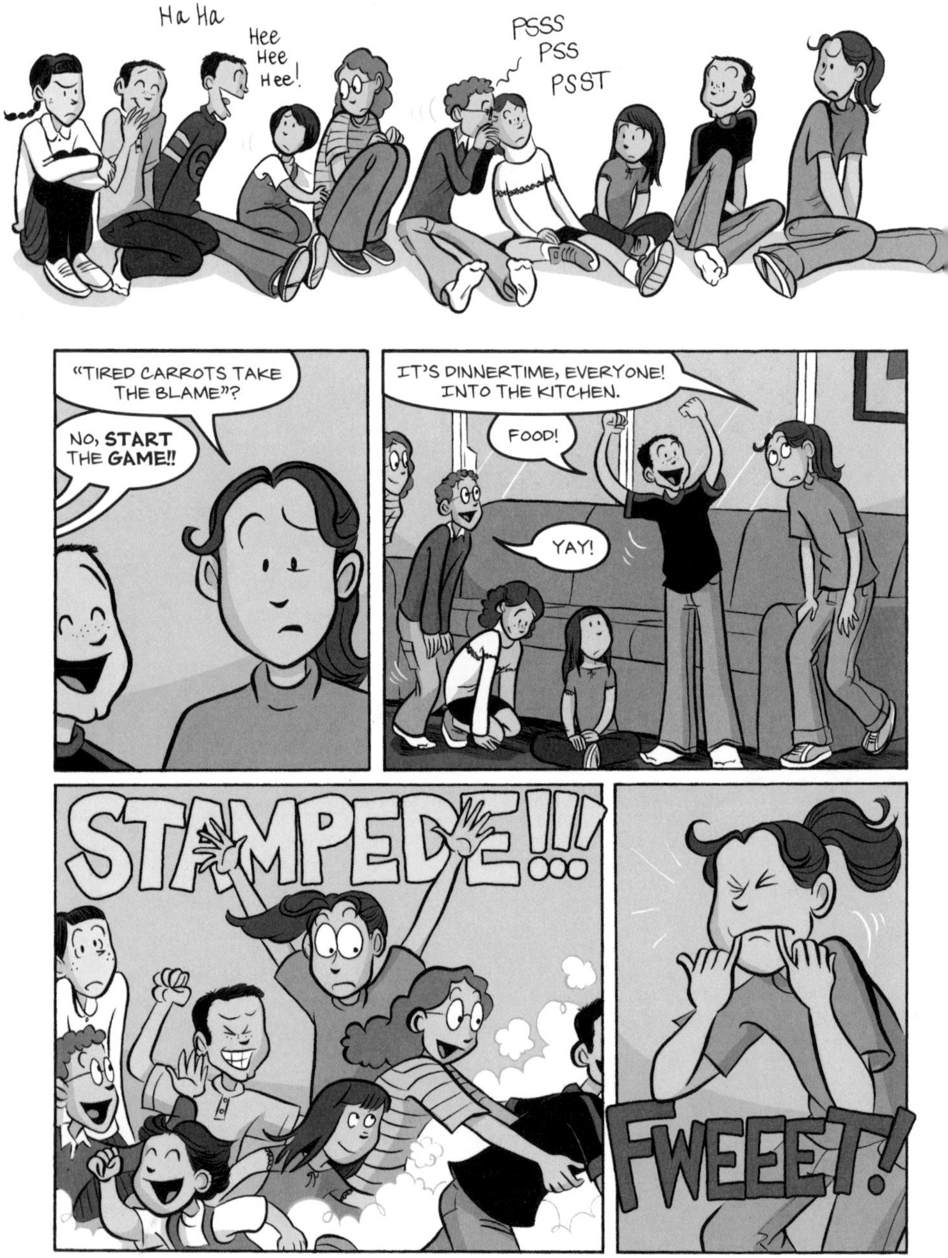
Ha Ha
Hee Hee Hee!
PSSS PSS PSST
"TIRED CARROTS TAKE THE BLAME"?
NO, **START** THE **GAME**!!
IT'S DINNERTIME, EVERYONE! INTO THE KITCHEN.
FOOD!
YAY!
STAMPEDE!!!
FWEEET!

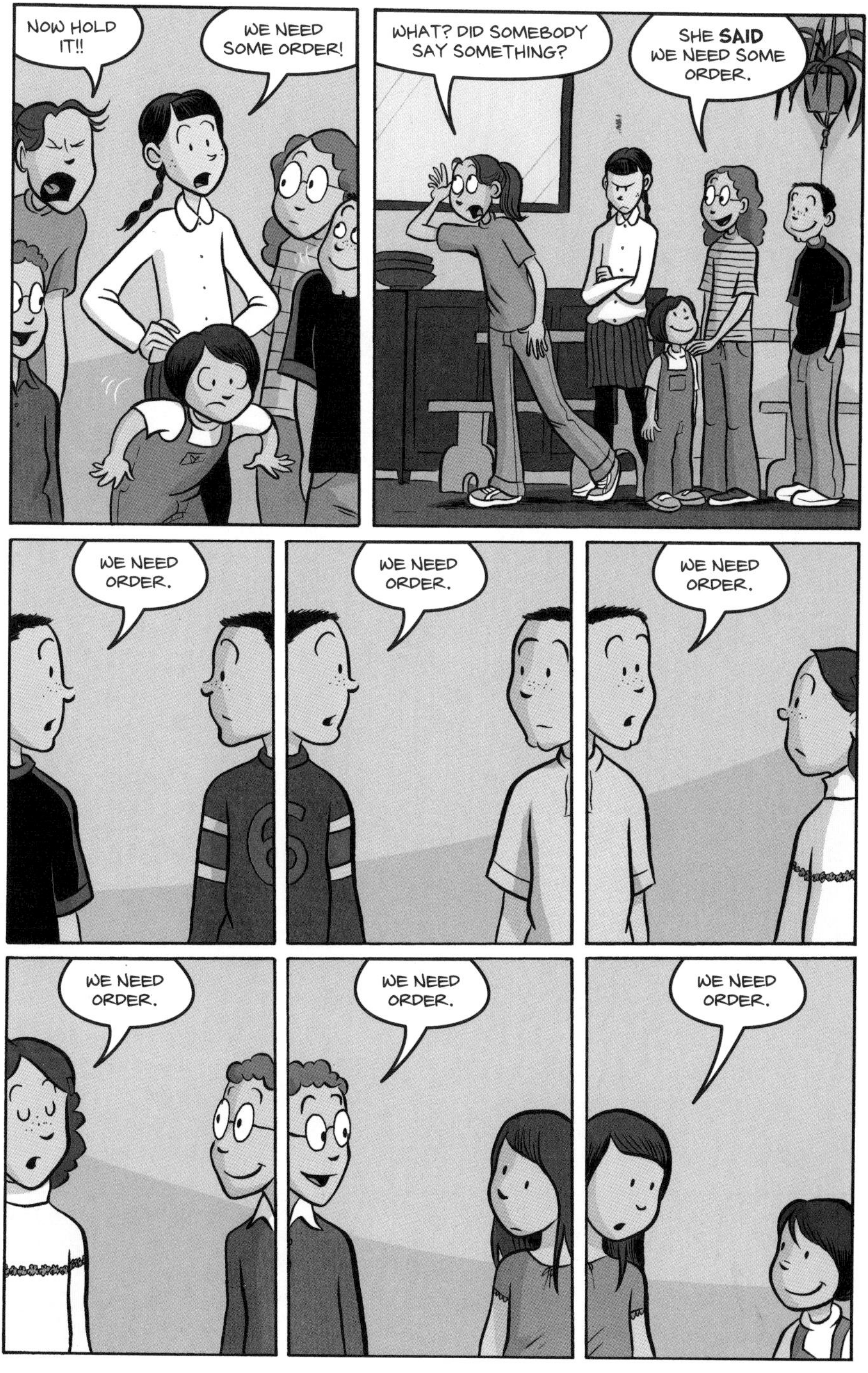
NOW HOLD IT!!
WE NEED SOME ORDER!
WHAT? DID SOMEBODY SAY SOMETHING?
SHE **SAID** WE NEED SOME ORDER.
WE NEED ORDER.
WE NEED ORDER.
WE NEED ORDER.
WE NEED ORDER.
WE NEED ORDER.
WE NEED ORDER.

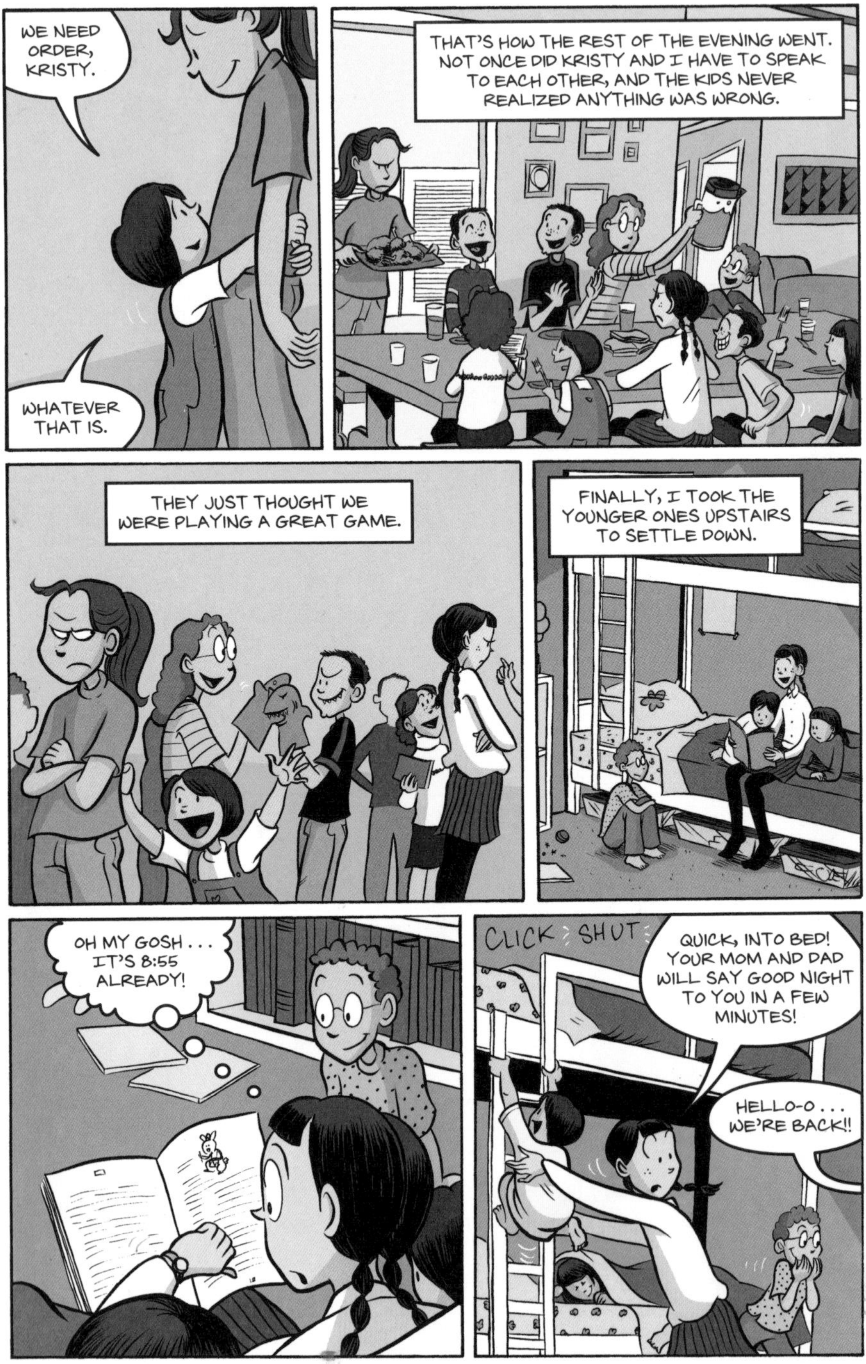
WE NEED ORDER, KRISTY.
WHATEVER THAT IS.
THAT'S HOW THE REST OF THE EVENING WENT. NOT ONCE DID KRISTY AND I HAVE TO SPEAK TO EACH OTHER, AND THE KIDS NEVER REALIZED ANYTHING WAS WRONG.
THEY JUST THOUGHT WE WERE PLAYING A GREAT GAME.
FINALLY, I TOOK THE YOUNGER ONES UPSTAIRS TO SETTLE DOWN.
OH MY GOSH . . . IT'S 8:55 ALREADY!
CLICK
SHUT
QUICK, INTO BED! YOUR MOM AND DAD WILL SAY GOOD NIGHT TO YOU IN A FEW MINUTES!
HELLO-O . . . WE'RE BACK!!

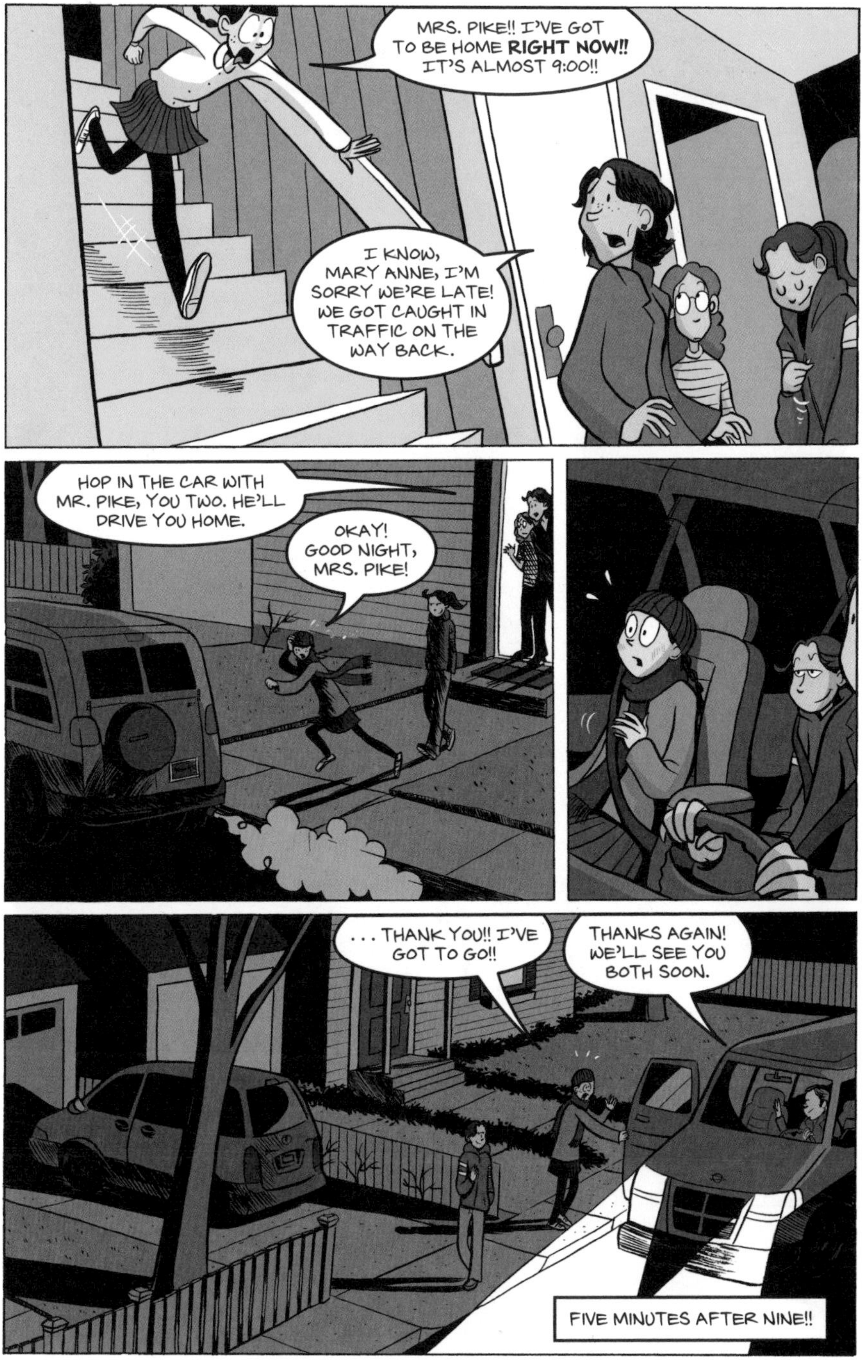
MRS. PIKE!! I'VE GOT TO BE HOME RIGHT NOW!! IT'S ALMOST 9:00!!
I KNOW, MARY ANNE, I'M SORRY WE'RE LATE! WE GOT CAUGHT IN TRAFFIC ON THE WAY BACK.
HOP IN THE CAR WITH MR. PIKE, YOU TWO. HE'LL DRIVE YOU HOME.
OKAY! GOOD NIGHT, MRS. PIKE!
. . . THANK YOU!! I'VE GOT TO GO!!
THANKS AGAIN! WE'LL SEE YOU BOTH SOON.
FIVE MINUTES AFTER NINE!!

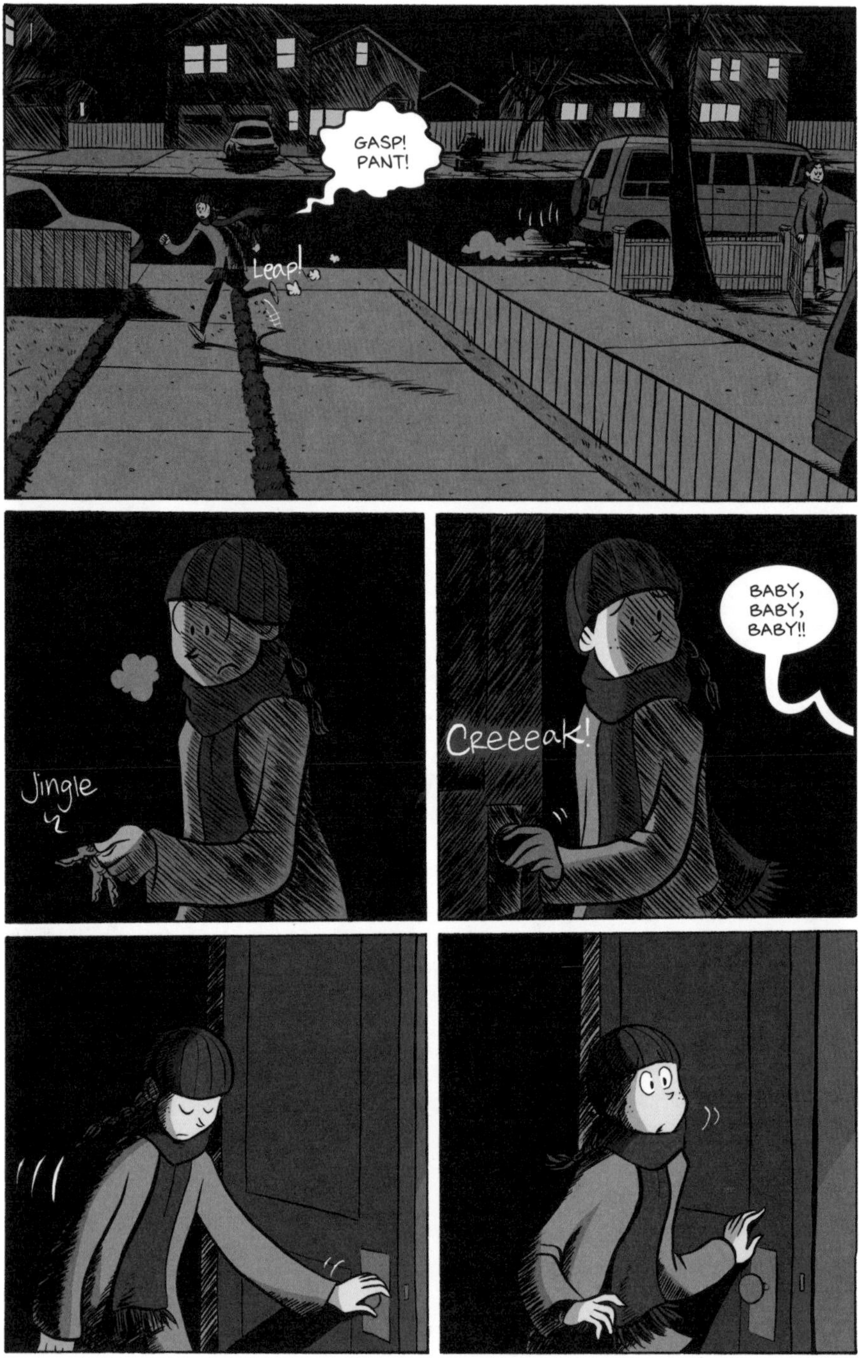
GASP!
PANT!
Leap!
Jingle
Creeeak!
BABY,
BABY,
BABY!!

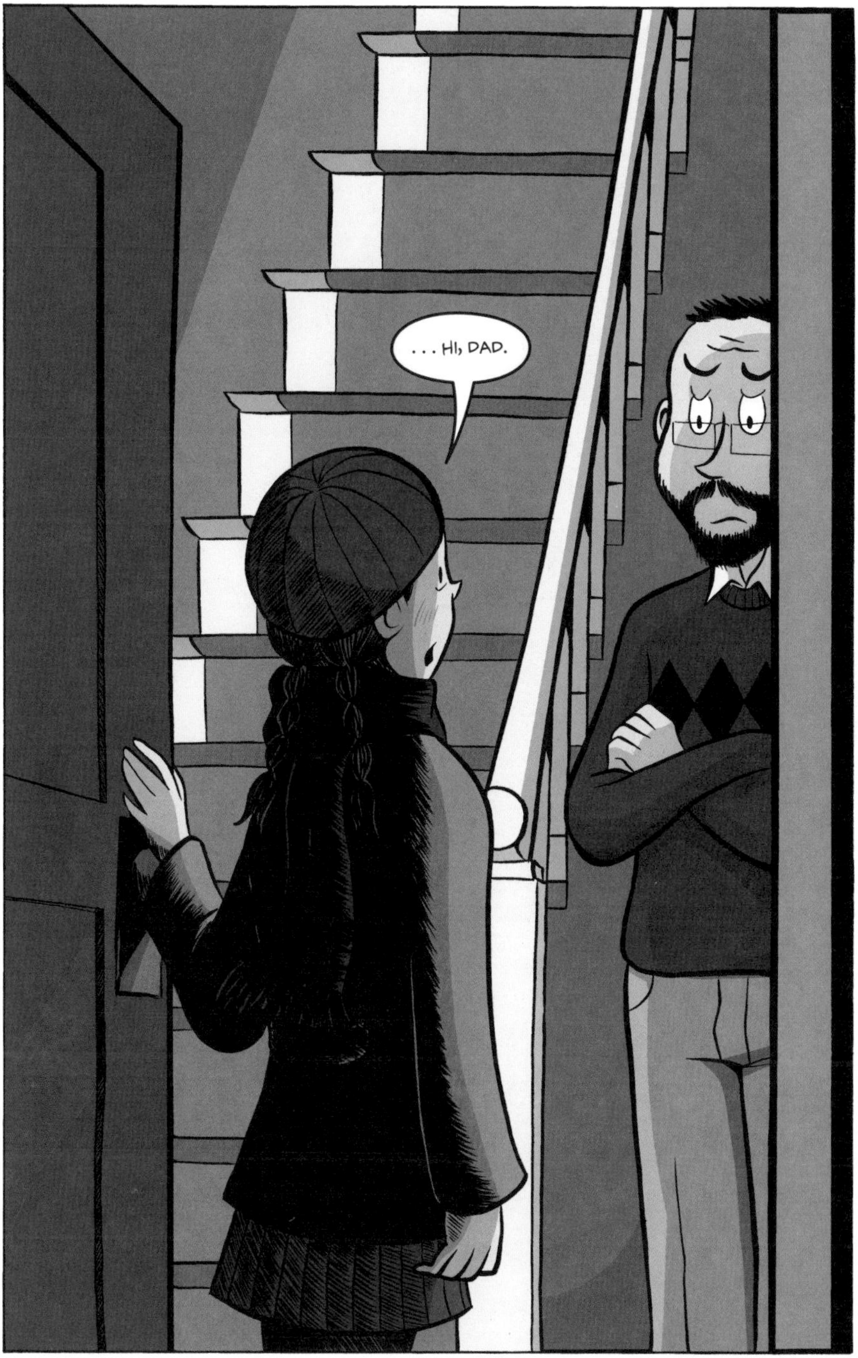
. . . HI, DAD.

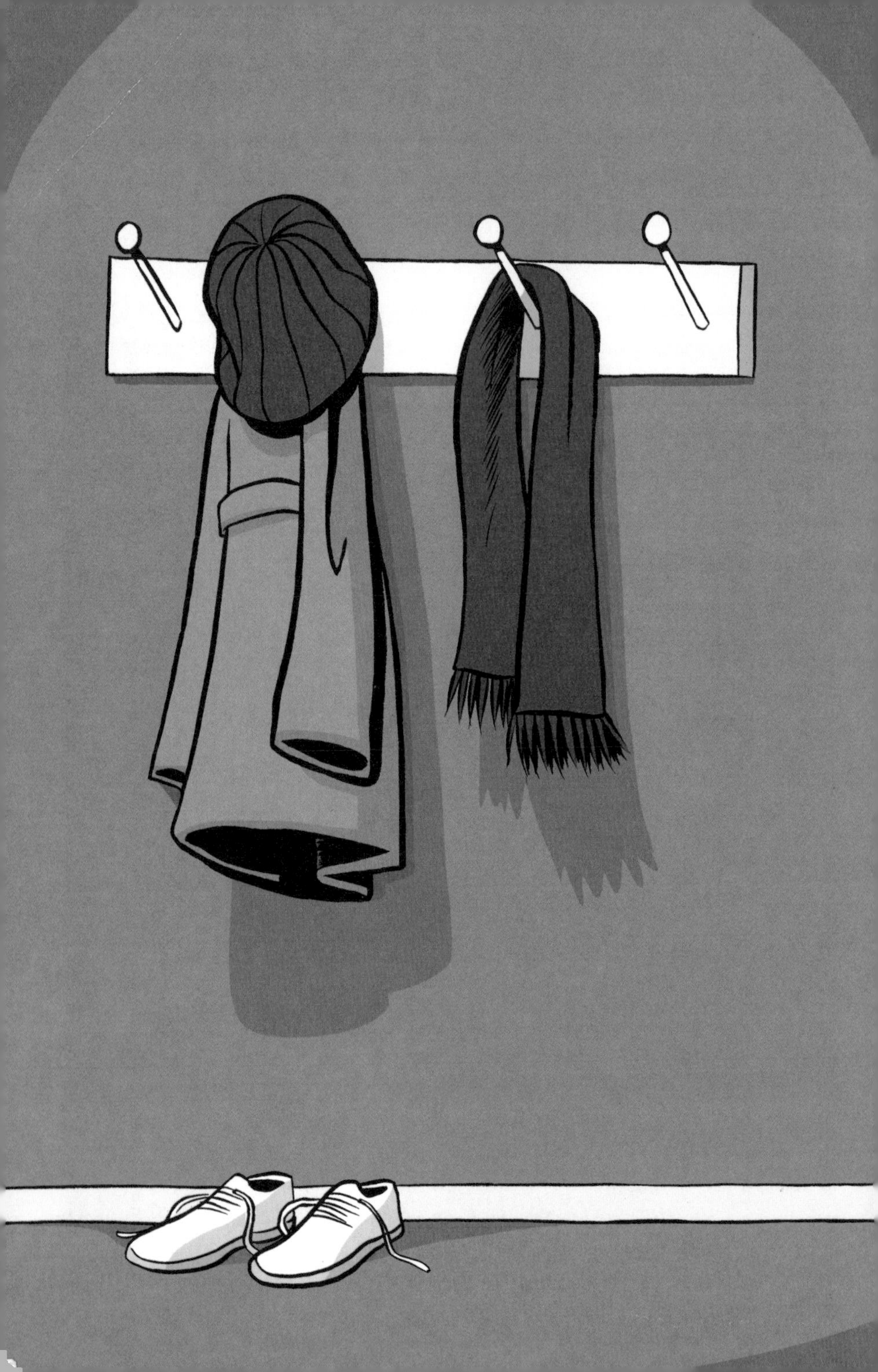

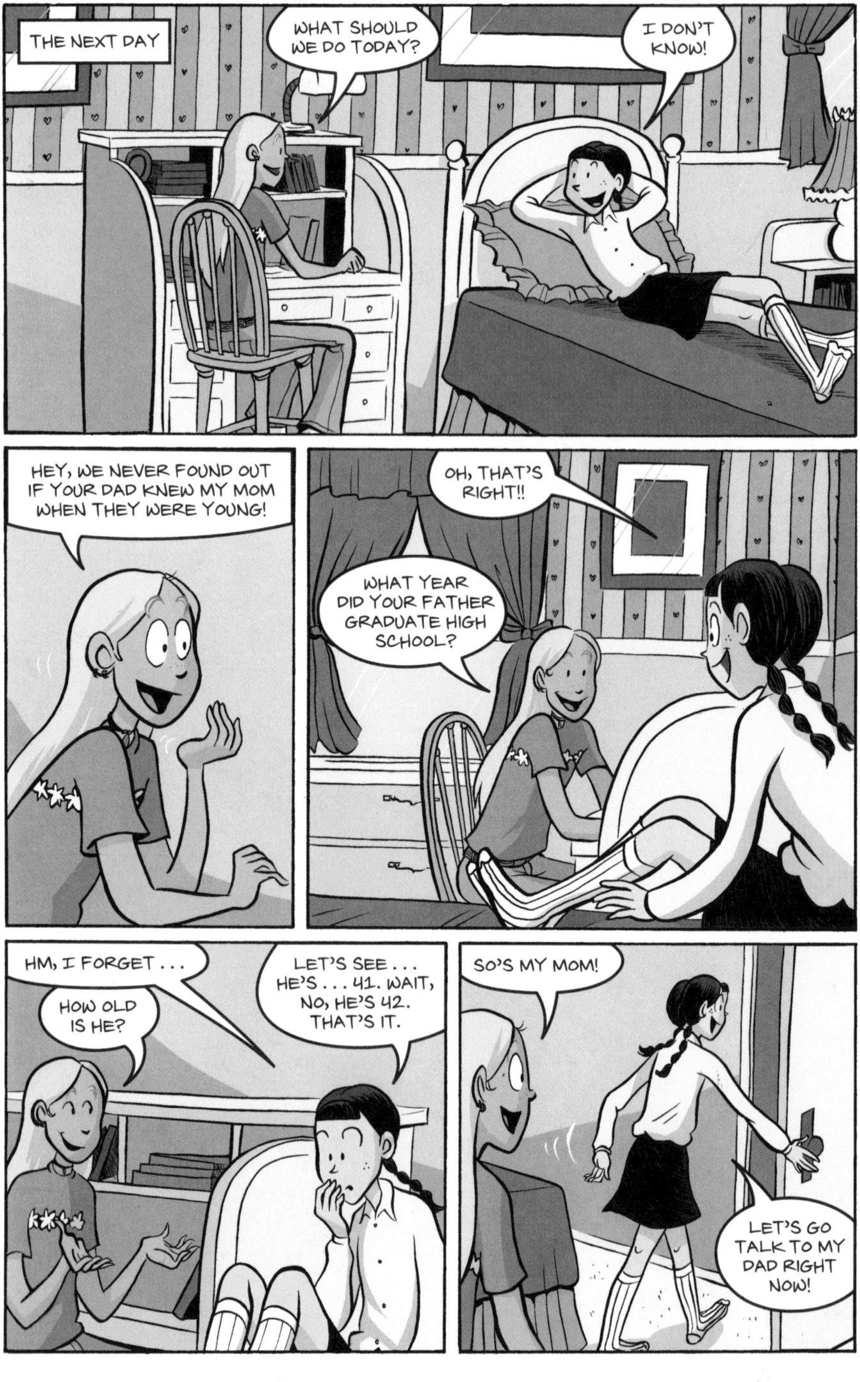
THE NEXT DAY
WHAT SHOULD WE DO TODAY?
I DON'T KNOW!
HEY, WE NEVER FOUND OUT IF YOUR DAD KNEW MY MOM WHEN THEY WERE YOUNG!
OH, THAT'S RIGHT!!
WHAT YEAR DID YOUR FATHER GRADUATE HIGH SCHOOL?
HM, I FORGET . . .
HOW OLD IS HE?
LET'S SEE . . . HE'S . . . 41. WAIT, NO, HE'S 42. THAT'S IT.
SO'S MY MOM!
LET'S GO TALK TO MY DAD RIGHT NOW!

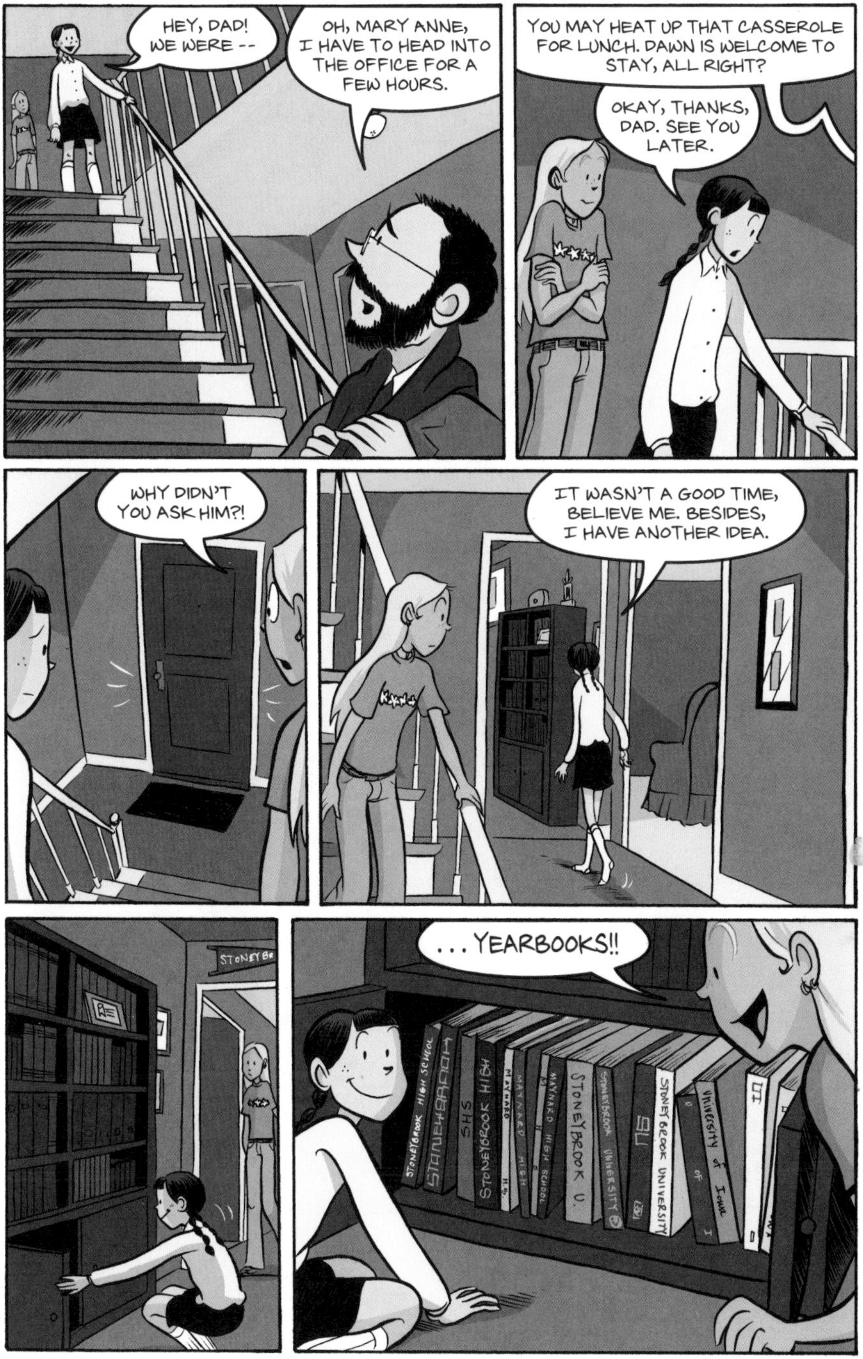
HEY, DAD! WE WERE --
OH, MARY ANNE, I HAVE TO HEAD INTO THE OFFICE FOR A FEW HOURS.
YOU MAY HEAT UP THAT CASSEROLE FOR LUNCH. DAWN IS WELCOME TO STAY, ALL RIGHT?
OKAY, THANKS, DAD. SEE YOU LATER.
WHY DIDN'T YOU ASK HIM?!
IT WASN'T A GOOD TIME, BELIEVE ME. BESIDES, I HAVE ANOTHER IDEA.
. . . YEARBOOKS!!
STONEYBROOK HIGH SCHOOL
SHS
STONEYBROOK HIGH
MAYNARD H.S.
MAYNARD HIGH
MAYNARD HIGH SCHOOL
STONEYBROOK U.
STONEYBROOK UNIVERSITY
University of Iowa

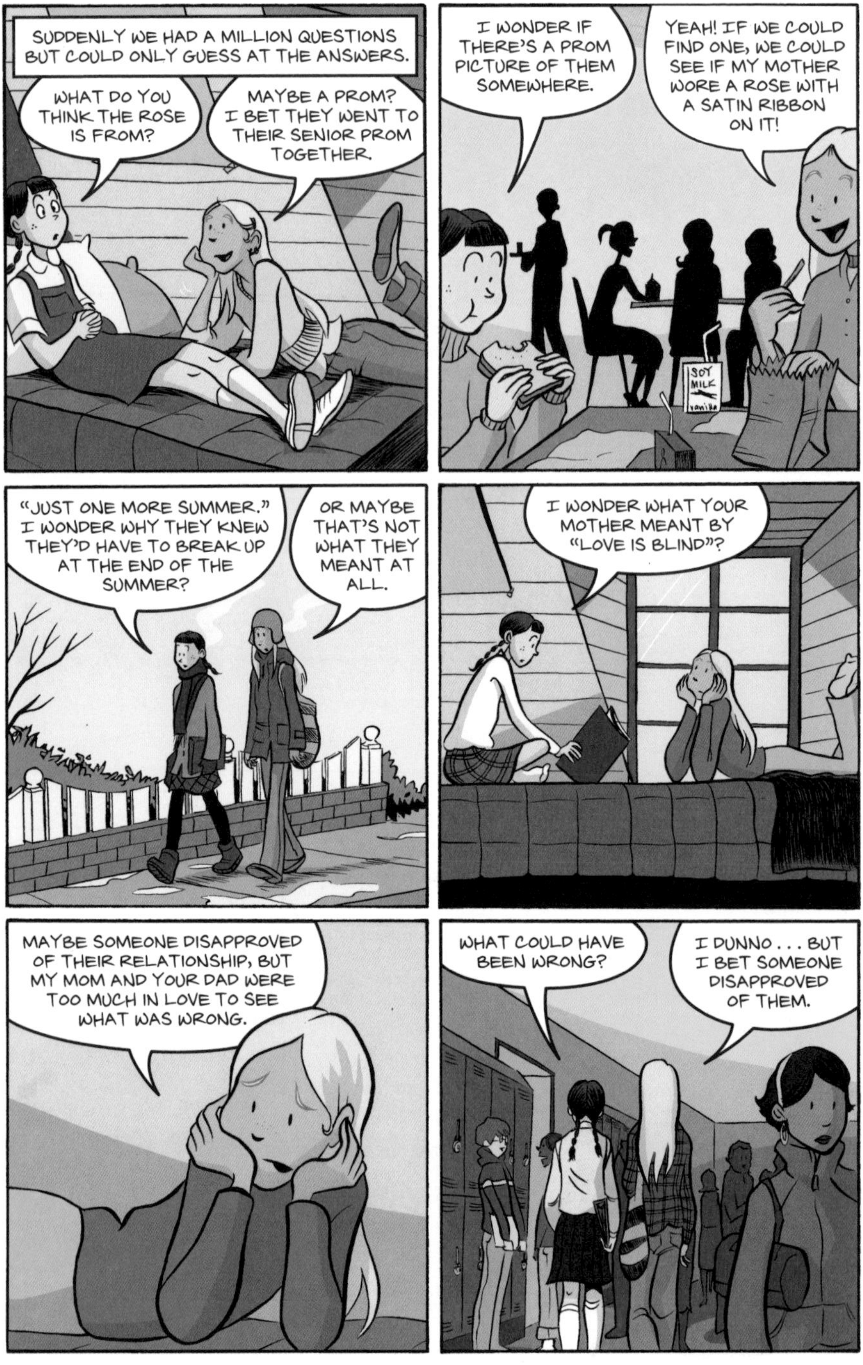
SUDDENLY WE HAD A MILLION QUESTIONS BUT COULD ONLY GUESS AT THE ANSWERS.
WHAT DO YOU THINK THE ROSE IS FROM?
MAYBE A PROM? I BET THEY WENT TO THEIR SENIOR PROM TOGETHER.
I WONDER IF THERE'S A PROM PICTURE OF THEM SOMEWHERE.
YEAH! IF WE COULD FIND ONE, WE COULD SEE IF MY MOTHER WORE A ROSE WITH A SATIN RIBBON ON IT!
SOY MILK vanilla
"JUST ONE MORE SUMMER." I WONDER WHY THEY KNEW THEY'D HAVE TO BREAK UP AT THE END OF THE SUMMER?
OR MAYBE THAT'S NOT WHAT THEY MEANT AT ALL.
I WONDER WHAT YOUR MOTHER MEANT BY "LOVE IS BLIND"?
MAYBE SOMEONE DISAPPROVED OF THEIR RELATIONSHIP, BUT MY MOM AND YOUR DAD WERE TOO MUCH IN LOVE TO SEE WHAT WAS WRONG.
WHAT COULD HAVE BEEN WRONG?
I DUNNO . . . BUT I BET SOMEONE DISAPPROVED OF THEM.

BUT THEN ON SATURDAY, SOMETHING HAPPENED TO KEEP MY MIND OFF OF OUR PARENTS, **AND** THE CLUB.

MARY

I HAD A SITTING JOB FOR JENNY PREZZIOSO. I GOT TO HER HOUSE AT 11:30.

DING DONG!

WHO IS IT?

IT'S MARY ANNE SPIER, YOUR BABY-SITTER.

STACEY HAD WARNED US ALL ABOUT JENNY IN THE CLUB NOTEBOOK, SO I WAS PREPARED.

ARE YOU A STRANGER?

NO, I'M MARY ANNE. MAYBE YOU SHOULD GO GET YOUR MOTHER.

THIS COULD BE A **VERY** LONG AFTERNOON.

HI, MARY ANNE. I'M MRS. PREZZIOSO, AND THIS IS MY LITTLE ANGEL, JENNY.

MY HUSBAND AND I ARE GOING UP TO CHATHAM FOR A BASKETBALL GAME.

HIS COLLEGE IS PLAYING THEIR BIGGEST RIVAL, SO HE'S VERY EXCITED.

READY, HONEY?

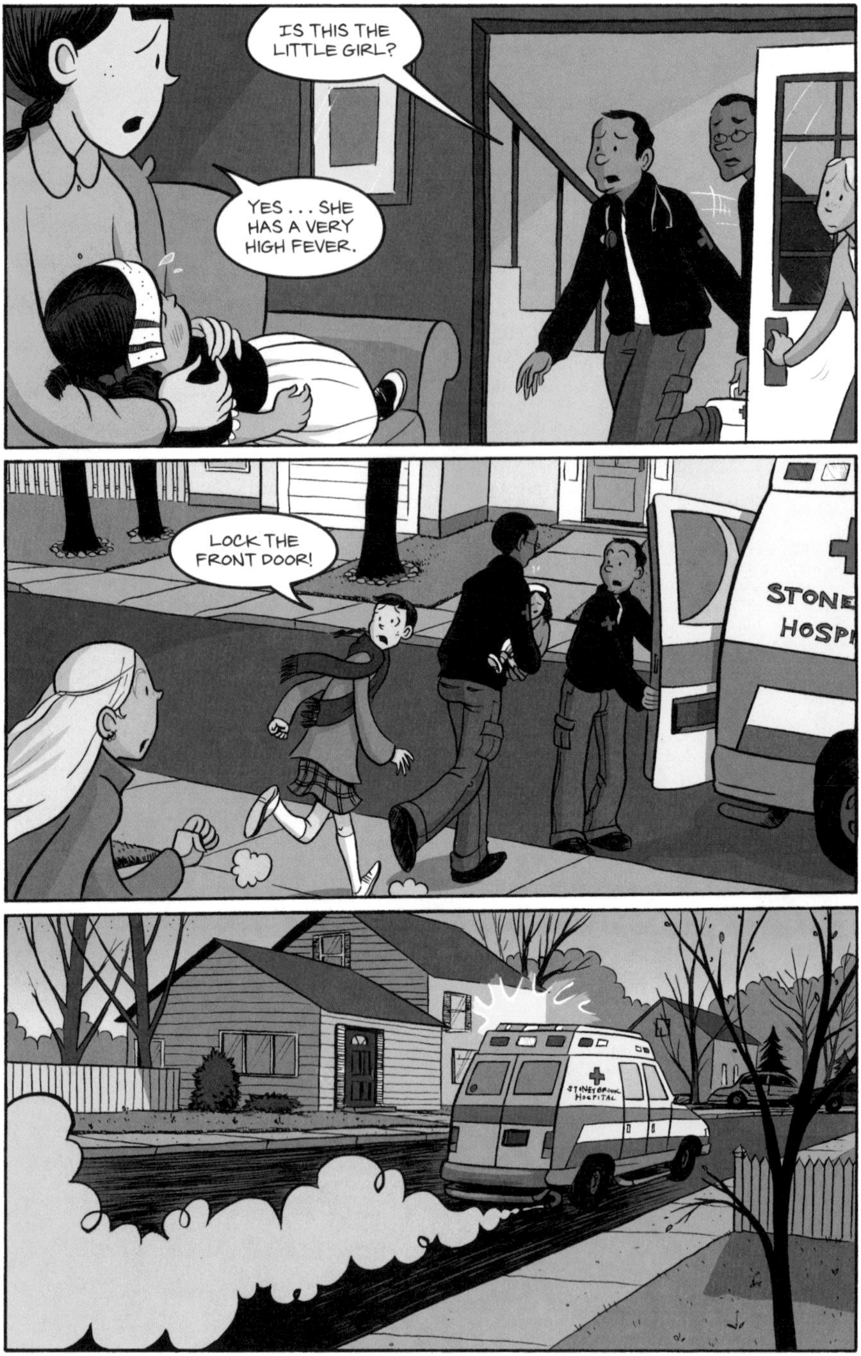
IS THIS THE LITTLE GIRL?
YES . . . SHE HAS A VERY HIGH FEVER.
LOCK THE FRONT DOOR!

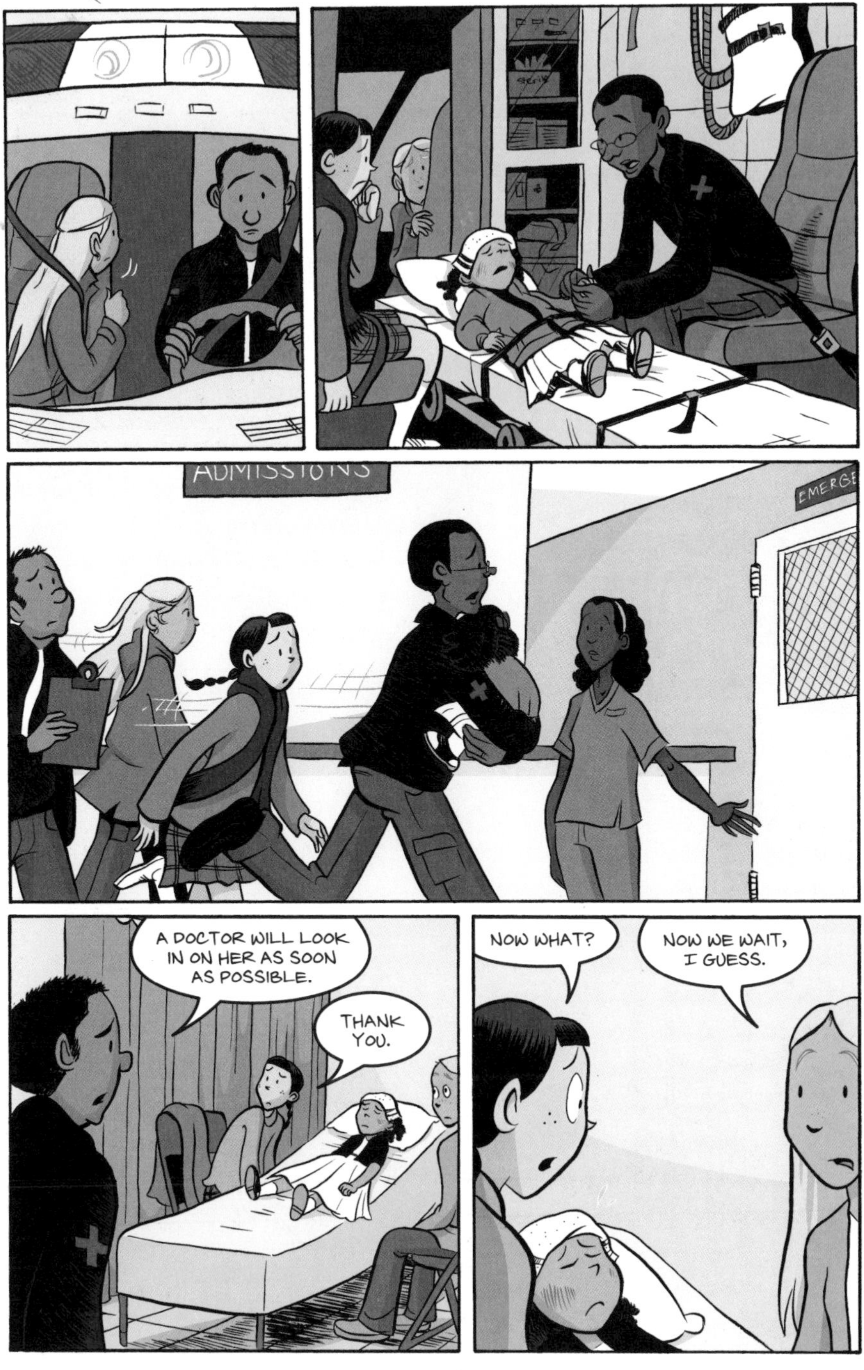
ADMISSIONS
EMERGE
A DOCTOR WILL LOOK IN ON HER AS SOON AS POSSIBLE.
THANK YOU.
NOW WHAT?
NOW WE WAIT, I GUESS.

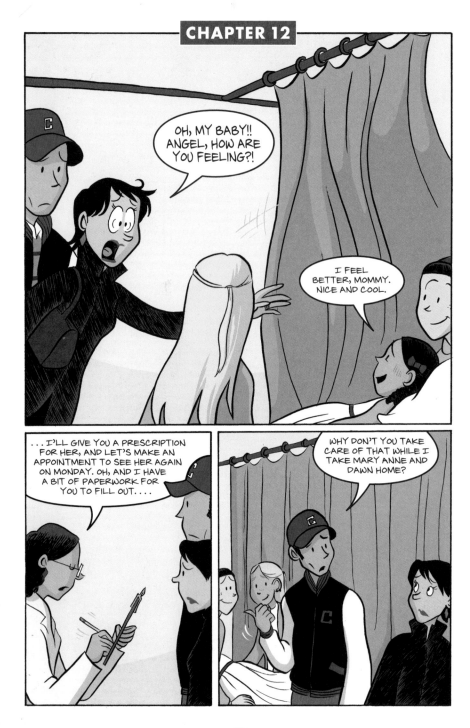

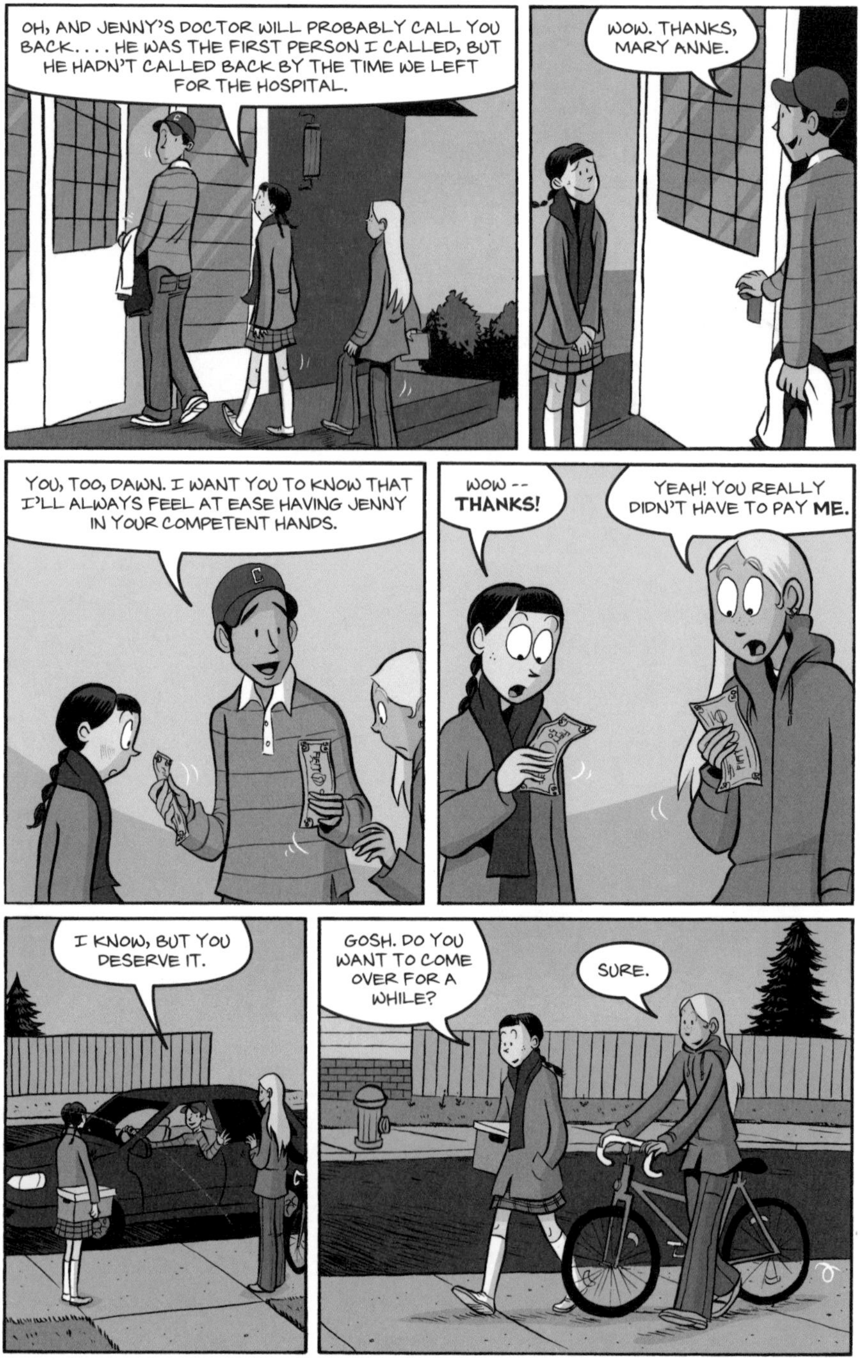
OH, AND JENNY'S DOCTOR WILL PROBABLY CALL YOU BACK. . . . HE WAS THE FIRST PERSON I CALLED, BUT HE HADN'T CALLED BACK BY THE TIME WE LEFT FOR THE HOSPITAL.
WOW. THANKS, MARY ANNE.
YOU, TOO, DAWN. I WANT YOU TO KNOW THAT I'LL ALWAYS FEEL AT EASE HAVING JENNY IN YOUR COMPETENT HANDS.
WOW -- **THANKS!**
YEAH! YOU REALLY DIDN'T HAVE TO PAY **ME.**
I KNOW, BUT YOU DESERVE IT.
GOSH. DO YOU WANT TO COME OVER FOR A WHILE?
SURE.

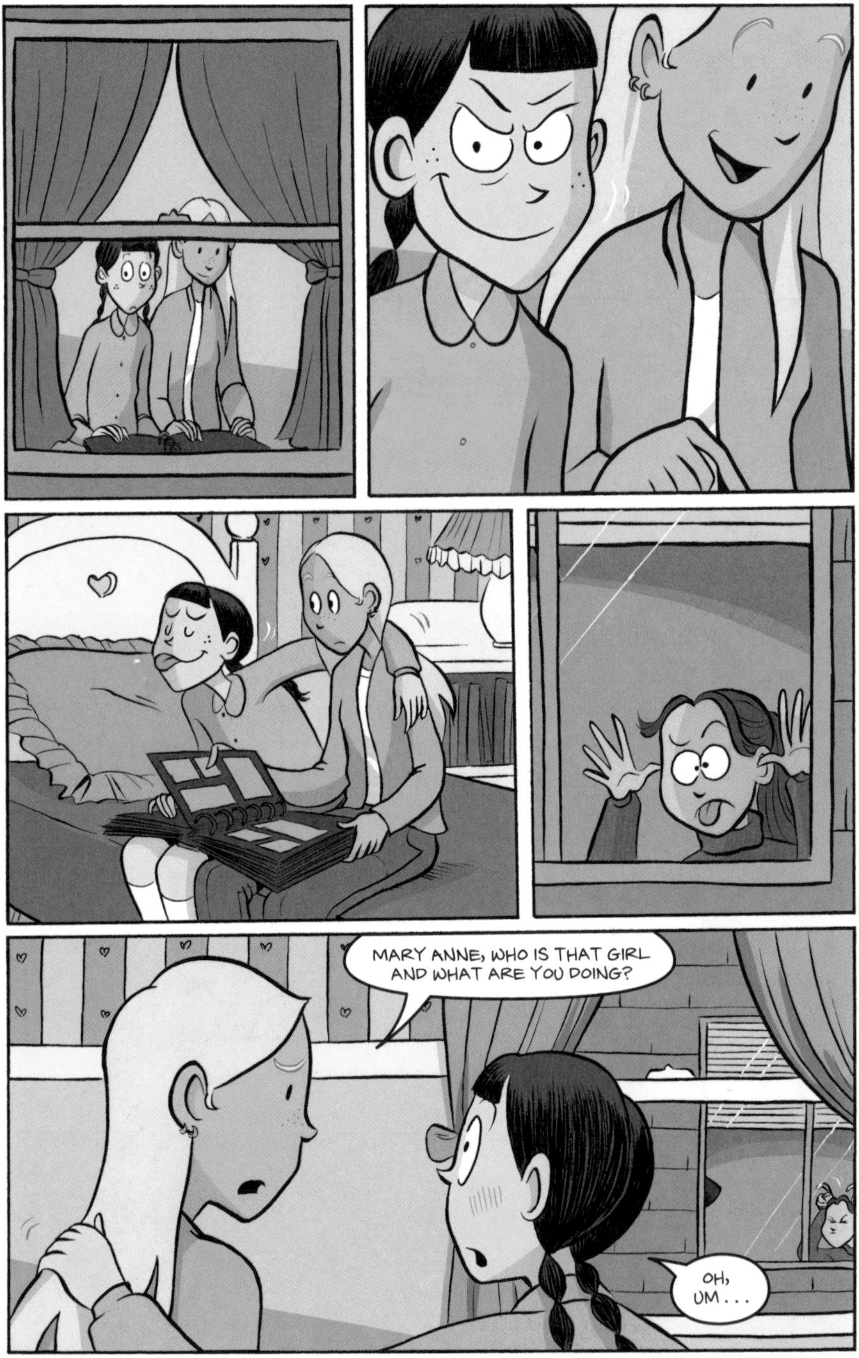
MARY ANNE, WHO IS THAT GIRL AND WHAT ARE YOU DOING?
OH, UM . . .

114

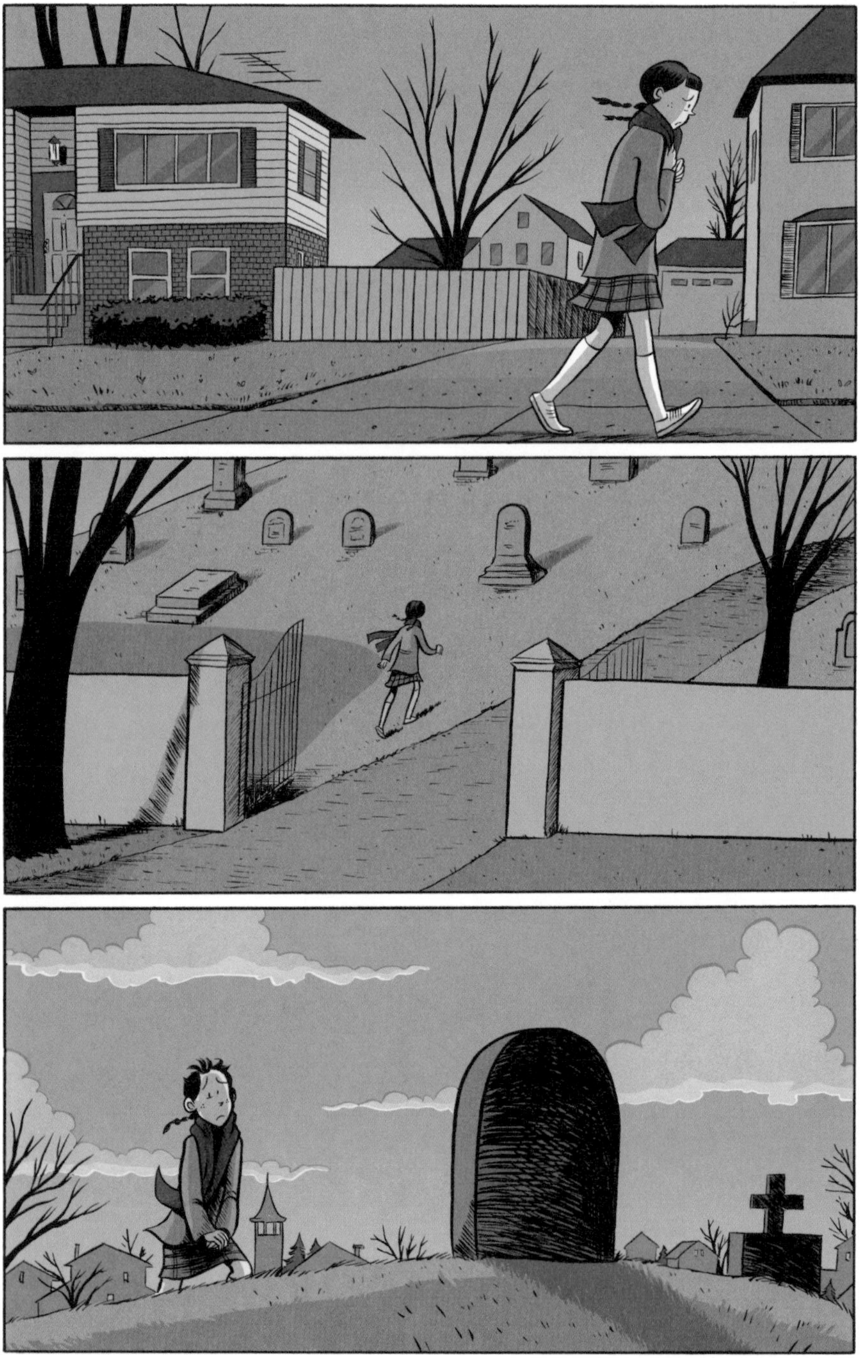

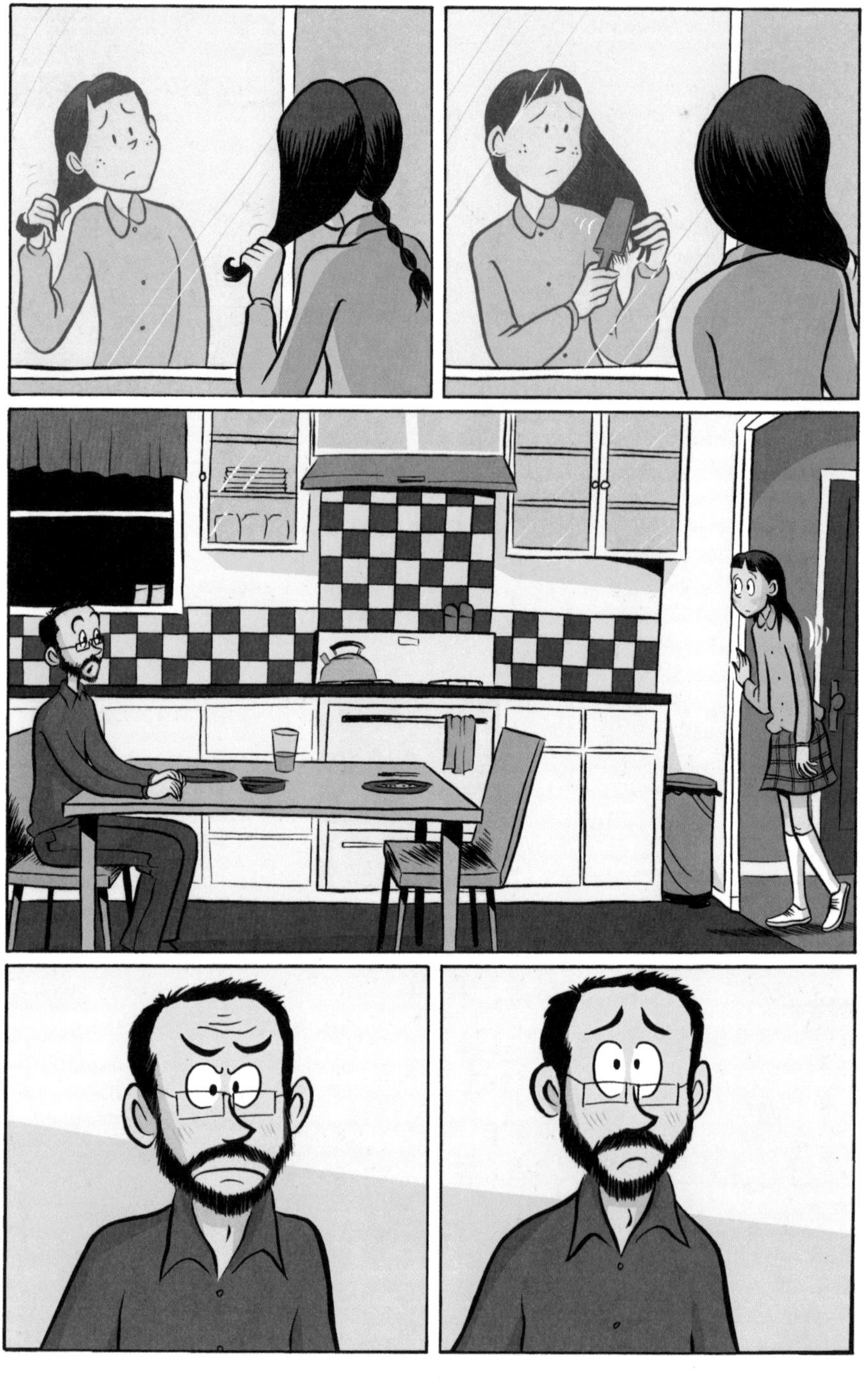

CHAPTER 13

Sunday, February 8

The members of The Baby-sitters Club have been enemies for almost a month now. I can't believe it. Claudia, Kristy, and Mary Anne – I hope you all read what I'm writing, because I think our fight is dumb, and you should know that. I thought you guys were my friends, but I guess not.

I'm writing this because tomorrow the four of us have to help out at Jamie Newton's birthday party, and I think it's going to be a disaster. I hope you read this before then because I think we should be prepared for the worst.

P.S. If anybody wants to make up, I'm ready.

Stacey

127

129

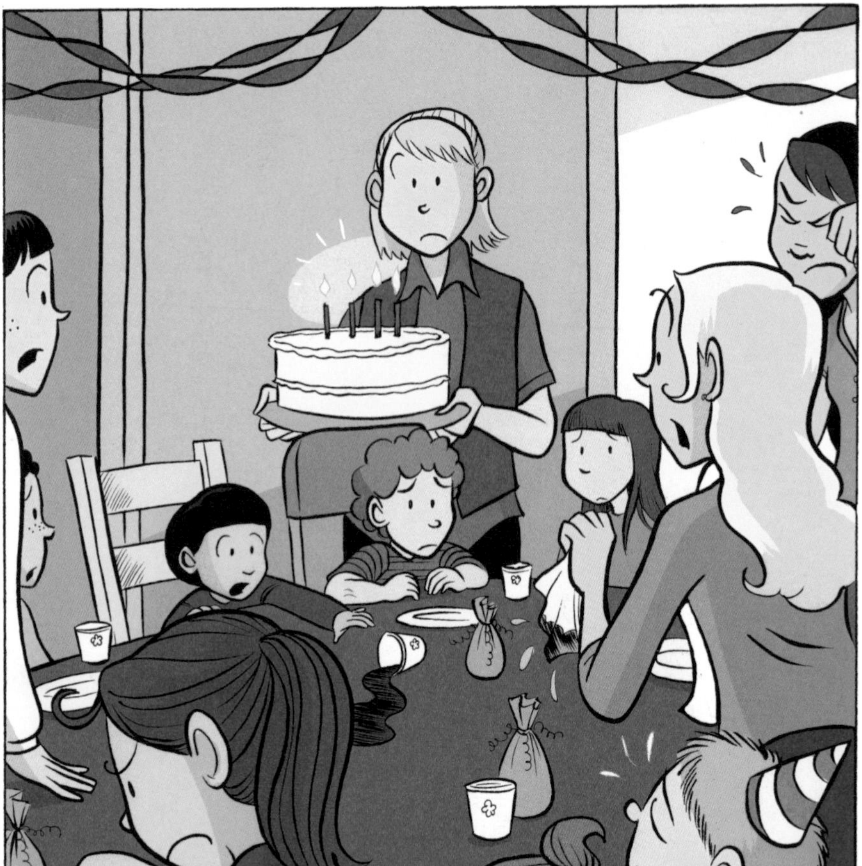

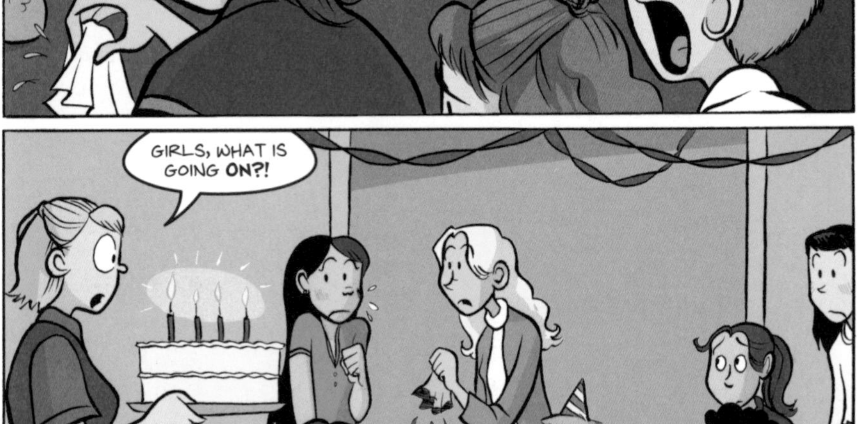
GIRLS, WHAT IS GOING **ON**?!

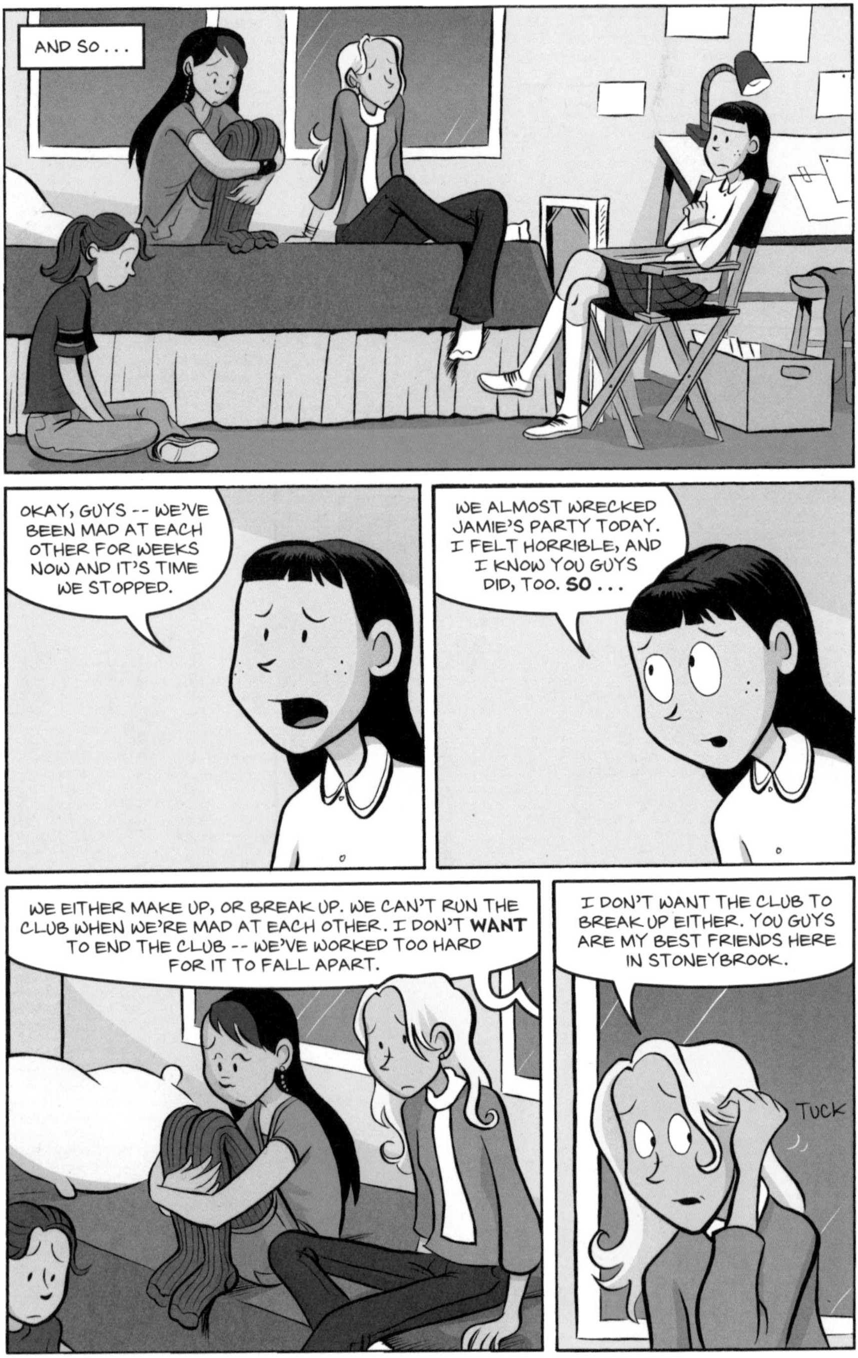
AND SO . . .
OKAY, GUYS -- WE'VE BEEN MAD AT EACH OTHER FOR WEEKS NOW AND IT'S TIME WE STOPPED.
WE ALMOST WRECKED JAMIE'S PARTY TODAY. I FELT HORRIBLE, AND I KNOW YOU GUYS DID, TOO. SO . . .
WE EITHER MAKE UP, OR BREAK UP. WE CAN'T RUN THE CLUB WHEN WE'RE MAD AT EACH OTHER. I DON'T WANT TO END THE CLUB -- WE'VE WORKED TOO HARD FOR IT TO FALL APART.
I DON'T WANT THE CLUB TO BREAK UP EITHER. YOU GUYS ARE MY BEST FRIENDS HERE IN STONEYBROOK.
TUCK

137

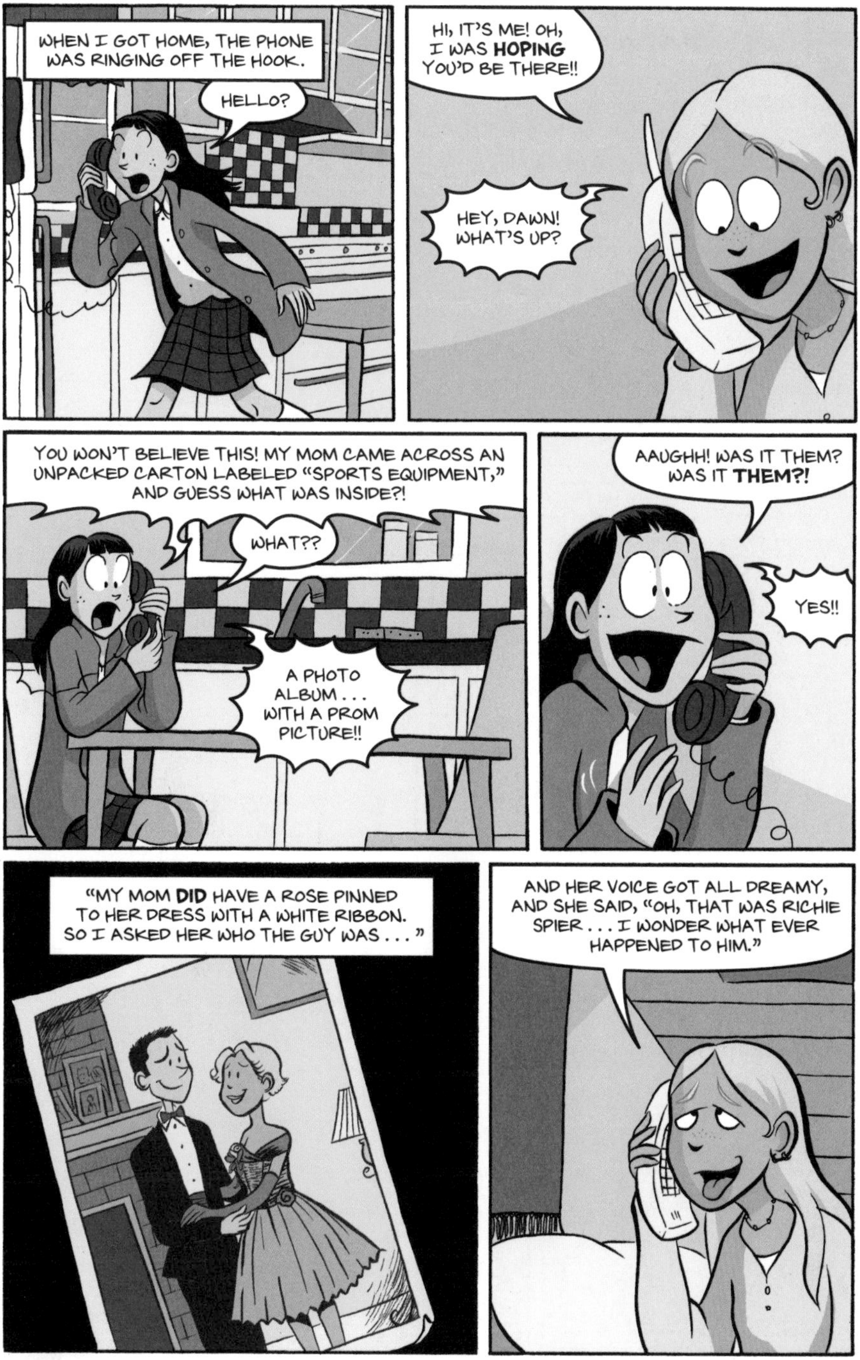
WHEN I GOT HOME, THE PHONE WAS RINGING OFF THE HOOK.
HELLO?
HI, IT'S ME! OH, I WAS **HOPING** YOU'D BE THERE!!
HEY, DAWN! WHAT'S UP?
YOU WON'T BELIEVE THIS! MY MOM CAME ACROSS AN UNPACKED CARTON LABELED "SPORTS EQUIPMENT," AND GUESS WHAT WAS INSIDE?!
WHAT??
A PHOTO ALBUM . . . WITH A PROM PICTURE!!
AAUGHH! WAS IT THEM? WAS IT **THEM?!**
YES!!
"MY MOM **DID** HAVE A ROSE PINNED TO HER DRESS WITH A WHITE RIBBON. SO I ASKED HER WHO THE GUY WAS . . . "
AND HER VOICE GOT ALL DREAMY, AND SHE SAID, "OH, THAT WAS RICHIE SPIER . . . I WONDER WHAT EVER HAPPENED TO HIM."

143

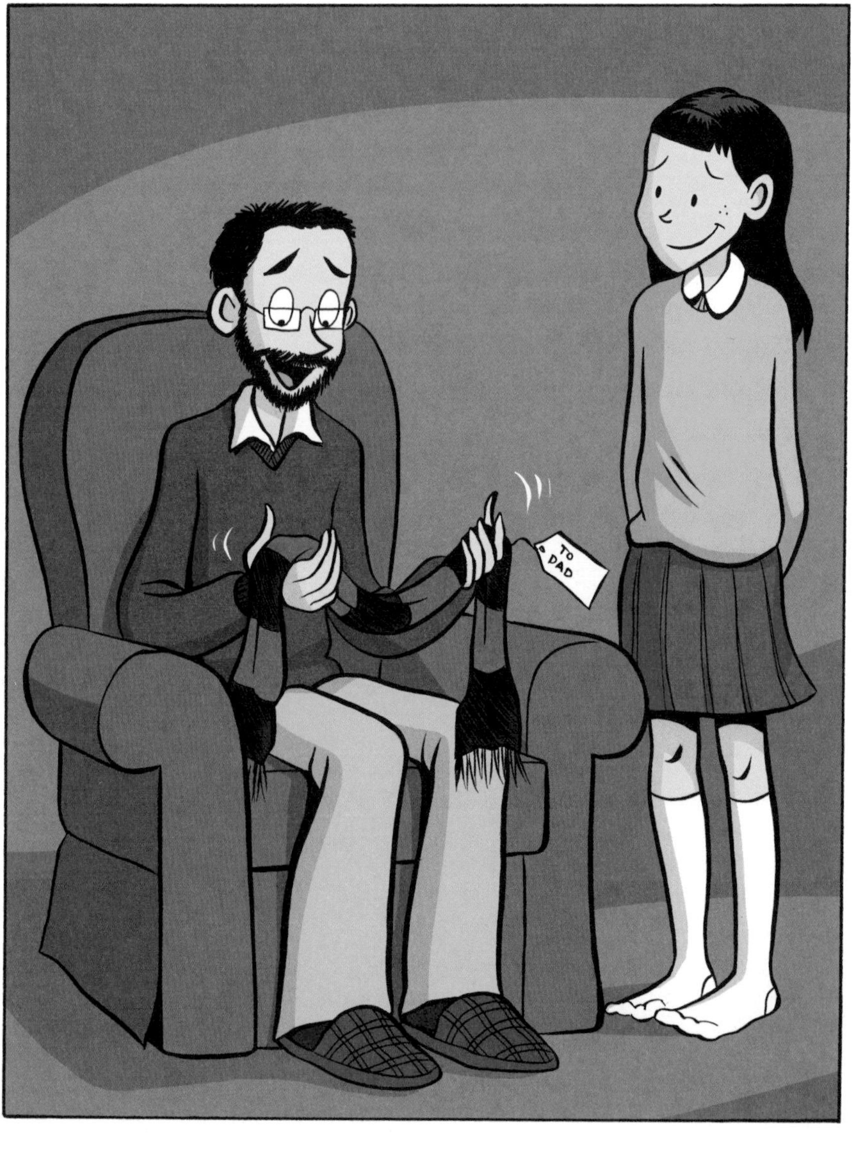
TO DAD

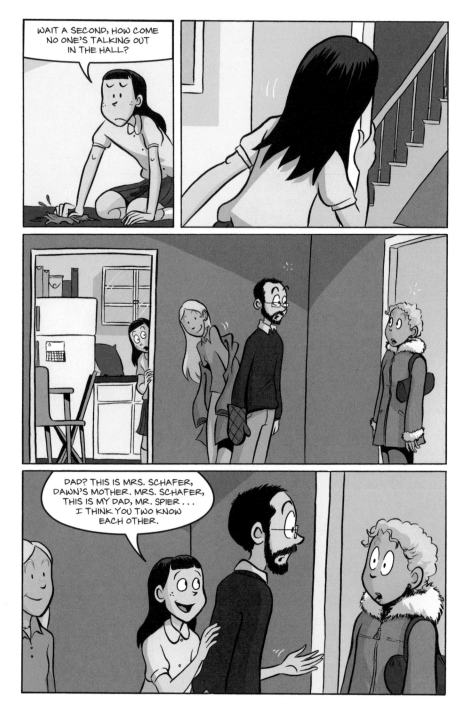

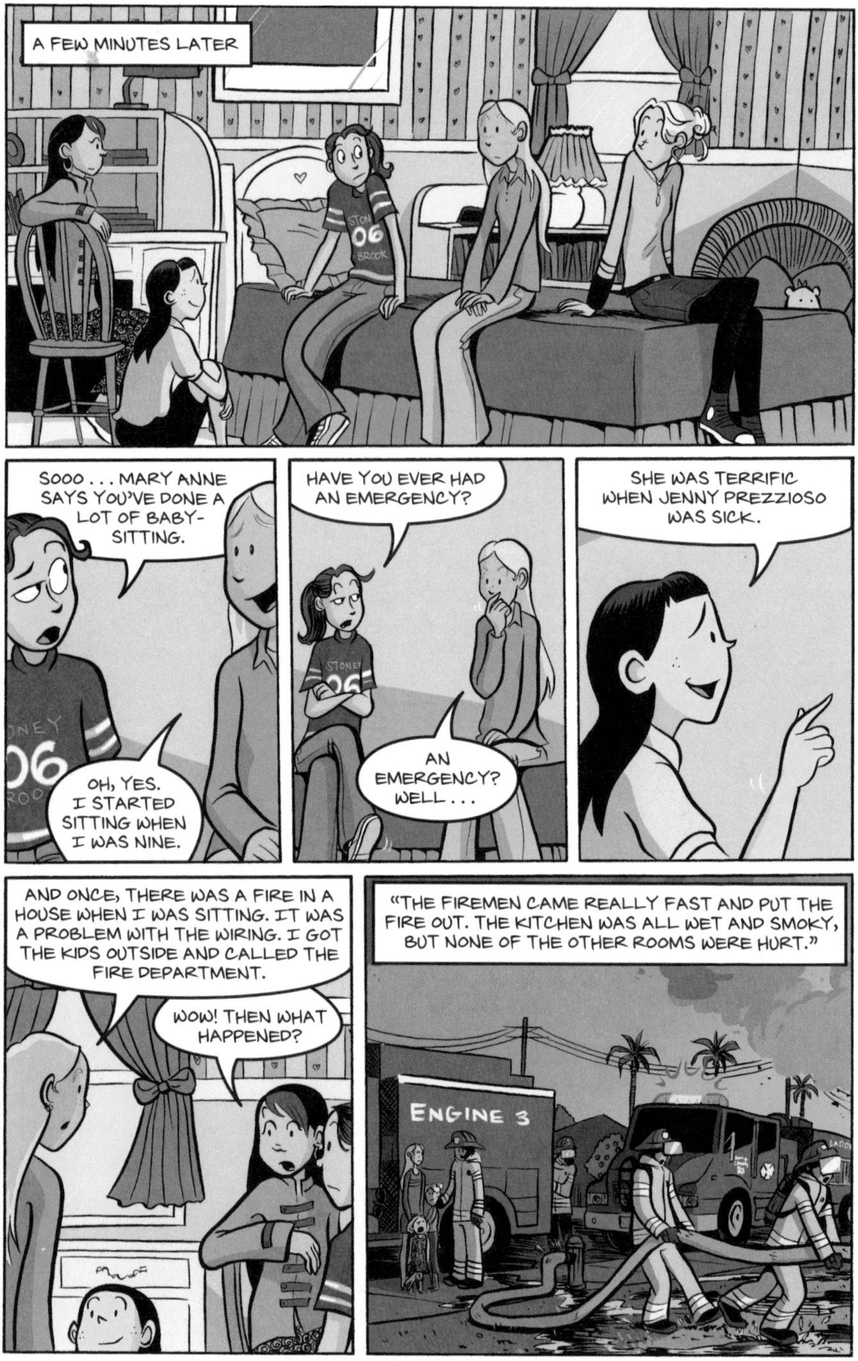
A FEW MINUTES LATER
SOOO . . . MARY ANNE SAYS YOU'VE DONE A LOT OF BABY-SITTING.
OH, YES. I STARTED SITTING WHEN I WAS NINE.
HAVE YOU EVER HAD AN EMERGENCY?
AN EMERGENCY? WELL . . .
SHE WAS TERRIFIC WHEN JENNY PREZZIOSO WAS SICK.
AND ONCE, THERE WAS A FIRE IN A HOUSE WHEN I WAS SITTING. IT WAS A PROBLEM WITH THE WIRING. I GOT THE KIDS OUTSIDE AND CALLED THE FIRE DEPARTMENT.
WOW! THEN WHAT HAPPENED?
"THE FIREMEN CAME REALLY FAST AND PUT THE FIRE OUT. THE KITCHEN WAS ALL WET AND SMOKY, BUT NONE OF THE OTHER ROOMS WERE HURT."
ENGINE 3

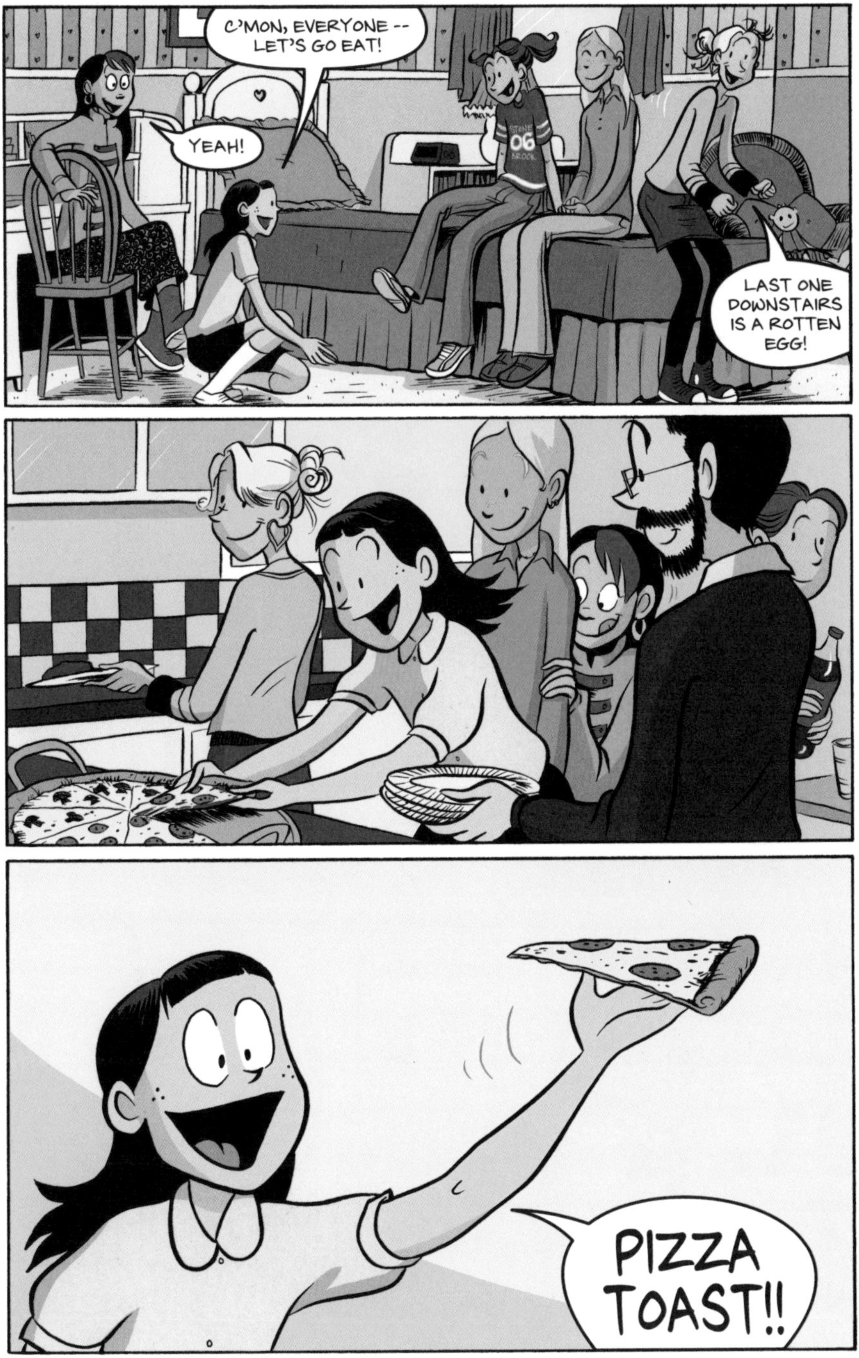
C'MON, EVERYONE -- LET'S GO EAT!
YEAH!
LAST ONE DOWNSTAIRS IS A ROTTEN EGG!
PIZZA TOAST!!

RAINA TELGEMEIER grew up in San Francisco, then moved to New York City, where she earned an illustration degree at the School of Visual Arts. She is the creator of *Smile*, a #1 *New York Times* bestselling graphic memoir based on her childhood. It won a Will Eisner Award for Best Publication for Teens, received a Boston Globe–Horn Book Honor, and has appeared on many state reading lists. *Sisters*, a companion to *Smile*, was a #1 *New York Times* bestseller and *USA Today* bestseller. Raina is also the creator of *Drama*, a #1 *New York Times* bestseller, recipient of a Stonewall Book Award Honor, and one of YALSA's Top Ten Great Graphic Novels for Teens.

Raina lives in Astoria, New York, with her husband and fellow cartoonist, Dave Roman. To learn more about Raina, visit her online at www.goRaina.com.